Coffin Nails and Salford Tales

ISBN: 978-1-907540-83-7

Published February 2018

Coffin Nails and Salford Tales

ISBN: 978-1-907540-83-7

Published February 2018

CHAPTER 1   THE DAY AFTER

As I walked into the Civic Centre the day after the night before, I didn't really know what to expect. I was greeted by my secretary, a lovely, nicely dressed in a beige suit, and a well-mannered woman.

Chapter One- The Reunion.

As I look back on the night that changed my life, I remember that I didn't really want to go to my 30-year school reunion. The venue was owned by a Manchester United player and the bar tariff was extortionate. I shouldn't really have even been crossing the threshold of the place.

As I got ready I feared that the passing of time would not have been kind to these people who I had been to school with. I put on a top that I had had for ten years. I was fully aware that these people who I hadn't seen for three decades would no doubt have gotten dressed up to the nines, and be wearing posh frocks and false smiles.

I arrived and said the obligatory hellos and smiled at people I didn't even remember, but straight away I sensed that there was warmth in the air and people were genuinely pleased to see one another. Polite chit chat developed into sincere inquiries about how people were doing, their families, their achievements, and the mistakes they had made in life. There was a sense that we all shared the same love of music, humour, and all had a desire to relax and reminisce. Polite smiles became warm, sincere smiles, and the pretentious atmosphere of the pub became insignificant. Having consumed the best part of 18 vodkas, it came to the point where my life would be changed forever.

I saw this guy (or bloke as we say in Salford) standing a little bit aloof from the rest of the crowd. He was just standing there with an arrogant swagger; taking it all in. Cocky bastard, I thought. I suddenly recognised his face as being a lad from school who had become a photographer. He looked very fashionable, unlike some of the other blokes that night. This made me think he must be gay. I associated being in gay company as meaning you were safe. They were not going try it on were they? And gays were more generous than straight men, so he might buy me a drink. I'll get onside with him later, I thought. Gay men tend to be a bit more thoughtful and better conversationalists.

The bar was crowded with an abundance of posers all talking, but saying nothing. The marble plinths and the ostentatious decor was straight out of a Footballer's Wives' room set. At that point I hadn't really taken much notice of the gay guy. I remember thinking that I might speak to him later if the company got boring. I overheard conversation with another member of the group and was surprised at what he was saying. He wasn't talking about his latest conquest in Canal Street and his voice was not what I expected from a man who was, for want of a better word, a chufter. I expected him to sound like Kenneth Williams, but he spoke more like Noel Gallagher after ten pints. At that point in the evening, Kathy, the lady who had organised the reunion, said she would order some food. I heard the grey haired gay say to his friend: "I'm not fuckin' staying here. I'm pissing off to the Holts, mate." That didn't sound very camp, I thought. "What a tight git he is! I've not much chance of getting a drink out of him!" I muttered to one of the girls who was standing next to me.

I know he was right; it was expensive. But he had made it so obvious that he was mean by saying it. He seemed the sort of man who was so tight he wouldn't even give a door a bang. I was to learn that he would make Scrooge's spending habits look like those of Elton John's.

I asked one of the group who he was and they told me his name was Williams; Simon Williams. I didn't remember him from school but everyone else seemed to. He was fairly quiet. He seemed to be a placid observer of everything that was going on around him. He was quietly absorbing it all. I thought he may have been a mute a first. Looking back I wish he was one.

I took less notice as I was getting more drunk and most of my energies were spent on trying to stand up straight and not say anything to offend anyone like, "You must have a bloody long paper round with no bike, mate." And "Time has not been kind to you has it?" or "Are they Botox lines on the side of your nose?"

We all left the homely atmosphere of the Ape and Apple and set off for a nearby nightclub. It was just the hard core drinkers who were left. There we were; a dozen forty-seven-year-olds who thought they were eighteen again.

We got to the club and I still hadn't spoke to the grey haired guy, but I had already sussed him out as being one of those that pissed off just before his round was due. We all approached the entrance of The Press Club. Some of the group were swaying and starting to slur remarks about how they were enjoying the evening and how glad they were that they had made the effort to come. We got to the door of the nightclub to find a bouncer checking everyone who entered.

He asked us where we worked as the club was strictly members only; intended for people that worked on the newspapers. I said nothing (on the basis that I wasn't working) but Williams mentioned straight off that he worked at the Manchester Evening News. Lying git, I thought. I assumed he was trying to get a free drink when he got inside. He looked the sort who would try and get 'ought for naught and then not even say thank you. Looking back now, that was an understatement.

I learned he literally would want anything for nothing. The bouncer asked the man called Williams for his ID card. I remember thinking, 'I wonder what the gobshite's going to say now, get out of that one!' He felt inside his pocket and said: "Do you know mate, I've left my wallet at home, I got it from Harvey Nicks and didn't want to risk getting it nicked, you know what these robbin' bastards are like in Manchester."

What a bullshitter, I thought. I knew there and then he must have been a United fan; they were all full of shit. If he wasn't a United fan, I would show my arse on the front door of the local Co-op.

I felt a little uneasy because it had been a long time since I had spoken to the remaining people, but this sense of unease disappeared as I talked to Joan, another member of the group, about our hockey days and how we had both liked the same boy. I noticed that Carol, a girl who, in my opinion looked a little cheap, was getting lots of male attention and even heard one of the men say: "Look at Carol. She still looks like a page three girl. By 'eck I wouldn't kick her out of bed for farting!" But Williams (as I was later to call him) wasn't really looking. He just stood, leaning against a small table clutching his pint. He reminded me of a cross between Steptoe and Rigsby; only better dressed. Part of me was pleasantly surprised that he was not as easily impressed with the "page three stunner." Page three my arse, more like page forty three of Reader's Wives. And that was on a good day.

Carol came over towards us. She had been flirting with more or less all the men in the group. Now she was approaching Williams. Not a chance love I thought. He's a batty boy. He would not be impressed with her overly blown hair and botoxed forehead. And then the moment came when I first spoke to him. The moment when my life would change forever. You know the crossroad moments in life? The moments where if you had turned left it would have had a totally different outcome than if you had taken the right turn. If I hadn't have spoken to him then you would not be reading this.

"You're a photographer aren't you?" I asked.

"Do I look like a fuckin photographer?" he replied.

My thoughts were that maybe he was not the person I thought he was and I was getting him mixed up with someone else. I couldn't really hear what he was saying; it was noisy. So, not wanting to appear rude I just nodded half the time.

He seemed to be getting a lot of female attention. I wasn't sure why. Perhaps they knew something I didn't. I wondered if he had made his fortune since leaving school and that explained his attraction. Eventually he asked me to dance and we got up on the dance floor.

I only ever get up to dance if I'm at the point of losing consciousness and that was the case that night. So, to be honest, I can't remember if he was a good dancer or not. But what I do remember is his indifference to Carol. She looked livid at the fact she was being ignored by a man. She tried to get him to dance with her but he ignored her advances and the more he seen her face turn purple with rage the more a kick Williams seemed to get out of it.

I became more impressed that his reaction to her was not like that of a normal bloke who would have quite easily have taken the opportunity of grasping what was in front of him. Williams seemed to find pleasure in that the fact she was appearing to be having a sulk and as much as I don't like to admit it, so was I. The fact that he was not like every other man in the group made me want to talk to him. But I couldn't hear a word he said. He seemed quite argumentative and let me tell you there's nothing better for a Salford girl than a challenge of getting the better of a bloke in verbal warfare. Little was I to know that I was never going to win the smallest battle against him.

I was not to know that he was wittier than Ali and his sarcasm was world class.

By this point the night was progressing into morning but I was insatiable. I wanted more ....lots more, more alcohol that is. He asked did I want to share a taxi as we both lived the same way. Tight fisted git I thought. But my thoughts were exactly the same; share the taxi fare and save a fiver. If I was lucky he might pay for all of it, but I thought there was more chance of Alex Ferguson retiring.

He said something about it being easier to get a taxi if you were with a woman. That was the first and last time he ever noticed I was a woman. And that was to enhance his chances of getting a taxi.

I tried hard not to be sick. But I thought if I was sick it would make room for more drink. I plucked up the courage to ask Williams what had been on my mind from the moment I started talking to him. I couldn't hold it back any longer and I needed to be satisfied.

I wasn't normally up front with a man but I took a deep breath and asked him: "You got any bevvy at yours mate?" before adding "Oh, and don't be thinking of any funny business either!"

He looked at me shocked and replied: "Oh, don't you be worrying about that mate, there'll be no funny business!"

I couldn't help but smile and think, Thank God for that!

Not in the habit of going back to strange men's houses I felt wary; but there was no need to be. He poured me a vodka (about a quarter of his own measure) but very quickly my bladder grew to the size of Wayne Rooney's head and I needed the toilet. When I went upstairs I noticed that his stair carpet needed hoovering but what I never noticed was the locked door, the half open entrance to the loft and a lingering smell of something sweet. I didn't know about his secret. I didn't know he had agricultural skills. But that, dear reader, is a whole new chapter.

Chapter Two- The Match

I had left early the next morning having slept on the settee. Williams had covered me up with a quilt and woke me up to drop me off at home. He looked rough; I on the other hand looked as fresh as a daisy. I remember thinking that I hoped I hadn't done anything. Then my mind started to remember things like his mantel piece being a disgrace, his kettle needed de-scaling and he really needed to upgrade his toilet rolls.

It was a little uncomfortable as he drove me home. I couldn't look at him and felt embarrassed that I had stayed at his house after only just meeting him.

He parked the car and said: "Look, you mentioned you've started some course or other, so you'll probably be busy and won't want to be bothered going out again, so I'll see you. I'll give you a ring in the week."

Yea, right, I thought. Won't hear a dicky bird that's for sure.

Tuesday came and with it a text. He called me Shazza for the first time; I replied with the name I would call him for the rest of our friendship. That name was Williams. I asked him did he mind being referred to by his surname.

He told me his mum called him Simon, His mates called him Si and the bizzies called him Williams. I decided to stick to Williams hoping it would wind him up.

I read the text which asked did I want my tea at his and he'd make me pasta with garlic bread. I answered telling him that I wasn't one to eat much (well, actually I do eat a lot but I didn't want to appear over enthusiastic about being fed and watered), but I looked forward to it.

At six o 'clock I received a phone call. The little shit, he's cancelling, I thought. But the next words were far worse than that. They were the words I had dreaded all my life.

"Do you want to go to Old Trafford mate?" he asked.

Fuck! What did I say? I feared getting a rash or a deep sense of nausea if I went within 30 feet of the place. Oh, fuck it! I thought. Just go. There's nowt on the telly. "Er, ok then", I said, after thinking about it for a minute. I'd never seen a Champions League game before and it would be an experience. But deep down I was worried that he would charge me for the ticket. I had never met anyone so tight and I didn't have the forty quid to pay him.

"Right, mate, pick you up in ten, hurry up and don't be late. It's a long fuckin' walk to the ground!" he shouted down the phone.

What a charmer, I thought. But I looked forward to watching a decent match, getting a programme, a Bovril and a Holland's Meat and Potato pie.

He picked me up. I was a bit embarrassed because he had been drunk the last time I seen him and now he was sober. We walked, and walked and walked. He was too tight to pay for parking near the Stadium of Dreams. Stadium of Dreams, my arse. Stadium of Shite more like. Eventually we got to the ground. He was panting and out of breath but still carried on lighting up his cigs at the same time as commenting on how he was going pack them in.

Well, readers, I was pleasantly surprised when we got to the ground. The seats were great and I couldn't have wished for a better view and Williams was quite polite and amusing. Then.....goal! Braga, the visiting team, scored. I was in fear of my life because I had the biggest grin on my face, I hid my smile behind my scarf. He was not best pleased. I commented on how United's defence were leaving gaps at the back on the left. His reaction was calm and cool. This was not what I intended. I thought my amateur comments would make him seethe but he didn't. But then the second goal went in.

"We're Man United and we'll score when we want!" he said.

You ain't gonna score on any level tonight, mate, I thought.

Half time came and I commented on how a nice cup of PG would go down a treat.

"You can fuck off!" he answered. "I ain't feeding the Glazers' pockets, Leave that to the Chinese and the Irish."

I remembering thinking how nice it was that he was embracing multi-culturalism.

"I gave FC United a tenner you know as a founding member!" he told me.

He seemed chuffed with his contribution to the rebel team and he was growing on me so I smiled and praised his generosity.

"So, are we not having a brew and a pie then?" I asked.

"Nah, not a fiver a go, mate. I only live in Swinton. You can wait and have a brew at mine!" he offered.

Who thought chivalry was dead? Me! Right there and then. Yet inside I was laughing. I was beginning to learn that with Williams there were no airs and graces. It was just genuineness all the way. I felt guilty (for about 2 seconds) that United were getting beat.

He asked me did I know the offside rule so I explained it more or less word for word from the FA Handbook. He said I was almost right. Almost right! What a nerve. Then, tragedy struck and United equalised within a space of minutes. Maybe, I thought, now he's in a better mood he might buy me one of the prawn sandwiches that everyone around us was eating. Not a hope in hell. But then something happened. A miracle. Williams was rustling about in his pocket.

I seen his hands fiddling and I started to panic. I could see a bulge in his pockets. A big bulge. It was a bit oddly shaped but beggars can't be choosers. I looked around where we was sat. There was no twenty-four-year-olds with miniskirts on. Cantona was not sat next to him. It wasn't me. I had no make-up on and looked as rough as 'owt.

The bulge got bigger.....and then of all of a sudden he got it out. It was a big one. It was a very big one. It was shiny and gold. It was my lucky day. It was a Crunchie quickly followed by a Toffee Crisp, then a Twix. But it was the Crunchie I wanted.

"Here, I've treated you", he said.

I smiled from ear to ear. That was the moment I knew he was a bit different. "Were they on offer by any chance?" I asked.

"Yea, you wouldn't have got one otherwise", he replied. "Buy one, get one free. In packets of four. Eight for two quid, mate", he said.

I was touched. The match ended 3-2. I was glad really, I would have felt awful if he had took me and United and got beaten. If you believe that reader, you'll believe anything. I was gutted.

The smirk on his face was unbearable. "You enjoy it, Shazza?" he asked.

"Yeah, great thanks. I had a good time", I said, muttering what a stingy bastard he was under my breath. I was dying of thirst. Mind you he said he would make tea so I guessed I wouldn't have to wait too long for a drink.

We got back to the car after the long walk from the stadium. On reaching the car he looked tired.

"Knackered me, mate!" he said.

He dropped me off and said goodnight. Charming, I thought. No brew, no pie, no programme, no pasta. But the Crunchie made up it. As the saying goes: It's the thought that counts. Not expecting to hear from him again I reflected on the fact that I had watched a Champions League match for nothing, as surprisingly, he hadn't taken the money from me for the ticket. But then on the Saturday I received a text. It was vague, much like him. It said: "Shazza, I'm in deep shit!" And that is when it all happened.

Chapter Three-The Rooftop Garden

I replied to the text nervously pressing the keys to ask him "What sort of shit? Is it just shit or heavy shit?" I pressed send waiting for the answer.

I had learned that week that Williams either replied to a text within seconds or days, depending on his mood. This time the reply came within seconds.

"Deep, deep shit, mate!" it read. Then another followed quickly. It read: "You better come round, mate."

Thinking he was going to reveal himself as a serial killer, an arsonist or even worse, a Tory MP, I drove there wondering what on earth compelled me to go. It wasn't his charm; that was non-existent. It wasn't the warmth of his living room, because he was too tight to put the fire on. Never the less, I parked up outside his house and knocked on the door.

"You better come in but I'm gonna check you for wires," he said.

Thinking he was getting a bit frisky, I hesitated about going inside.

"I couldn't phone you last night cos Swinton cop shop confiscated my phone!" he told me.

I was caught between feeling shock at his involvement with the police and a sense of being happy that there was a genuine reason for not getting in touch, however dodgy that reason was. "What for?" I asked.

"You'll never believe it, mate. They've got me down as some sort of Billy Big Time cannabis dealer!" he said. He seemed to be deeply insulted at the accusations. "Do you know what I'm worried about mate?" he said.

"What, mate", I asked.

"My seventy year old mum. Oh the shame of it!" he said. "I can just imagine it. All my mum's mates running round waving the Salford City Reporter about asking her "Is that your Simon on the Before the Bench page?" That's what bothering me mate, nothing else."

I asked how they could accuse him of such a thing asking him how they could make such a mistake.

"Oh, it ain't a mistake, mate. I had thirty plants up in the loft. All growing nicely as well."

I asked him what sort of plants were up there, thinking he may have done an agricultural course at night school and was perhaps cultivating some crocus bulbs in the dark to sell on the market. I was an innocent girl having been brought up in Seedley, a posh part of our home city. In hindsight my naivety must have appalled him. Before he answered it suddenly dawned on me. He was growing weed in the loft. Then something else dawned on me. I had slept not ten feet away from his plants when I had stayed that night. The bastard. "So, what happened last night when they came?" I asked.

"Well, let me tell you, Shazza. It's quite funny really, mate," he said. And that was when he started to recount the events of the previous night. "Well, I was sat watching Corrie when the door went. It was the man from Eon stood there with two coppers. I had a funny suspicion what it was about," he said.

At this point I thought the best plan was to say turrah and go and get a McDonalds. Stress always made me want to eat. He carried on telling me what had happened.

"So I asked them what they wanted. The Eon man said he was here to investigate the sudden upsurge in my electrical supply and why I had used only used 2 weeks of electric in three years. He then asked to see my meter. I knew there and then they had me banged to rights. Well, Shazza, the next thing they traced the wire to my back bedroom where my plants were growing contently. Totally ignored the 'Do not disturb' sign, mate. No fuckin' respect."

I wondered why I had not noticed it when I stayed the week before but realised that 28 vodkas and distorted vision had something to do it.

"They frogmarched me out into the street. The fuckin' curtains were twitching all over, mate. Bet no fucker in this street watched the end of Corrie, that's for sure! Bet they all had to watch it on catch up, nosey bastards."

"So what happened after that?" I asked, fearing the worst.

"Well, they emptied the loft. My pension fund gone. Gone. In the back of four vans. Four fuckin' hours it took 'em. Cleared me right out!" he said, as though he was the innocent victim of an index linked pension fund.

I told myself to leave the house and never come back. But I ignored the voice in my head. Quite frankly, I wanted to know what happened next. So I stayed. Then he continued.

"They woke me up at half seven to interview me. I looked at the two coppers who came and I thought I'll have some fun here with these two. They introduced themselves. The WPC started first by asking me stupid questions as though she thought I was going to slip up. I looked at her and thought I've got a daughter older than you. Everything she asked I turned the question back to her. I'll tell you what was said: "How much do you spend on beer, Mr Williams?" "How much do you spend, love?" Do you like nice holidays?" "Don't we all, love?" "How much do you spend on clothes, Mr Williams?" "How much do you spend, love? I bet you like nice clothes!"

Williams told me it became like a game of table tennis and there was only gonna be one winner. He carried on with the tale.

"That's when the drug sergeant stepped in. As soon as he started I thought I'd give him a run for his money. So every question he asked I replied, "No comment."

At this point in his story, I realised he was accustomed to

this sort of thing. The voice on my shoulder told me to go but it was more interesting listening to him than watching the EastEnders omnibus and let him carry on.

"The copper asked who had fiddled the electric as it was a professional job. Then he asked did I admit to growing plants and how did I know what to do. I told him" the internet" He asked me if the two larger plants that they had taken were the mother plants. I asked him how he knew about that, then he replied "the internet!" We all laughed as though there was a little bit of mutual respect in that one. They bailed me and that was when I had to do the walk of shame, mate."

Never having heard of the walk of shame I asked him what it was. Dreading the answer I sat down having the feeling that it was going to be a very long day. I remembered that when I first seen him I thought he was a gay photographer. How wrong could I be. I recalled how at the reunion he had just observed his surroundings and not really mixed very much. In hindsight I realised he must have been wary of GMP watching him.

"The bastards took my phone, my laces and my belt. I had to walk all the way home with a little brown property bag. I felt a right twat, I can tell you."

"Why did the take the laces off you?" I asked naively. "In case I think of doing anything stupid, mate," he said.

When he said that I thought if I stayed any longer I was the one who was stupid. The good conscious on my shoulder told me to wish him all the best and fuck off out of there, while the bad conscious told me to stay and listen to more. Against my better judgement I decided to stay. I was a bit shocked because I didn't know why. I had always thought that if I was faced with a moral decision that I would always take the right option. But something had told me that he was a decent sort.

Life had taught me not to make hasty judgements of people. Life had also taught me that things were not black and white but there were shades of grey in between. He had made me laugh telling me what had happened but I sensed that he was worried about telling his mum. I had only known him a few weeks but my instincts were not to turn my back on him. What were a few plants? And he had only borrowed the electric from Eon. I left and said if he ever needed anything just to ask. I was quite touched he had felt he could trust me and tell me what had happened. My offer of help was taken up a week later. Well, not help exactly. But I'll tell you what happened next.

Chapter 4-Buried Treasure

A week had passed and I had not heard from him. I imagined him sat in his loft lamenting his lost pension fund. I wondered if he had done something stupid but then decided he was not the sort. I wondered how he had gone on and if he was okay but by the end of the following week I decided it would be best if I didn't hear from him. Then on the Friday evening about ten o'clock my phone notified me of a text. I read the message which said, "Shazza, get us some ciggies mate and drop 'em off." I looked for a please at the end of the text but could not see one. I tutted but laughed inside and set off to get the cigs.

When I arrived he opened the door and said: "You alright, mate?"

"Yeah, here's your ciggies Williams. Three pounds twenty six please", I said. I'd like to say he said thanks for getting them and here's some money for your petrol. But he didn't.

"Do you want to come in for a vodka? Go on come and have a quick vodka", he offered.

It was then, when I stepped inside, that I noticed a teenage boy sat on the settee drawing. He told me that it was his son and it was then that I saw another side to this man that had already shocked and surprised me. I was to find that night he was as good at nurturing his children as he was his plants. He didn't nurture the vodka though. It didn't stay in the bottle long enough.

He gave me a drink and I noticed that the measure was a marked improvement in the one he had given me two weeks before. He must be mellowing I thought.

As time wore on I noticed he was getting a little bit drunk.

He became a little bit loose tongued. It was then he started to tell us about his hidden treasure.

"Will, if anything ever happens to me, there's fifty grand hid in a black bag buried near your nana's shed. But don't tell your nanna," he said.

I noticed his son's eyes light up. So did mine. The bad conscious on my shoulder told me to try and find out where Williams' mum lived.

He continued to tell his son the details: "its three paces away from the fishing gnome and four paces away from the bird bath," he said.

Will asked him what he had to do with it if anything happened.

"Well, son," he said. "There's twenty grand for you, and fifteen each for Sam and Nicole."

I could see Will calculating it to see if it added up as Williams was slightly worse for wear at this point, but it all added up okay. I was wondering if they would notice a couple of grand missing. I'd seen a nice bag in Selfridges that I liked and I could do with some new knickers. I could get ten pair for five quid on Bury market.

Will looked as though he wasn't that bothered but Williams knew it was making his son curious and carried on telling him about his hidden stash. Will was listening intently with a mixture of innocent interest and an admiration for his father that was a bright as the twinkle in his eyes when he had heard about the money.

I realised quite quickly that the story was probably a big fib. But I wasn't entirely convinced and made a mental note to go and check out the sheds in his mam's road as soon as I found out her address. I had become accustomed to Williams' tall stories but humoured him and when I saw his son hanging on his every word I realised why he told them. It was to make people happy by making them laugh. Then Williams asked me did I know he was related to Robbie Williams from Take That.

Oh God I thought, just humour him. "No, I didn't" I replied.

It was then I was to hear the words I would hear at least twice a week every week after that. He lifted his top up and said: "Look at that chest! This chest is chiselled from Salford's finest marble!"

I was a little embarrassed because his son was there but I thought it would be rude not to. After all he had asked me to look. And my dad had always told me to do as I was told. I looked, expecting it to look like a typical 48 year old man's chest. He wasn't wrong. It was, in fact, finely chiselled. I didn't know whether it was lifting slates that had done it or illegal steroids, but I wasn't complaining.

I looked at Will and pretended to be unimpressed. Probably aware of the cost, Williams did not put the fire on that night, even though winter was getting near. But he didn't need to because the warmth between father and son filled that room and as I left I began to realise that my newly found friend was worth his weight in finely chiselled marble.

Chapter 5- A hidden talent

Well sometimes things happen that are best left unsaid. For the men reading this little tale it would be considered unimportant. For the women it is more so. But I'll choose to skim the details and condense three weeks into a few paragraphs. It is safe to say that some days I thought I knew my new mate Williams inside out. I asked him questions as I was curious to know what made him tick. He was unlike anyone I'd met before and I was curious to know what was inside his head. I knew there was a lot inside it; it was just a little jumbled up. Some days I didn't know him at all. I thought he had me sussed out fairly quickly. I knew that he knew, he could more or less be certain that with me what he seen was what he got. He could trust me with his life. But all I'll say is that now, as I type this story, he knows he can. But one night he didn't and it cut to the core. Deeply.

Some things are best left out of print; like Giggs' affair, the details of Gareth Thomas' sex life and the goings on in the House of Commons and so are the details as to the reasons why our friendship was temporarily severed. It was only through my pig headed perseverance that it was repaired. Williams would never have tried to. Sometimes we don't like to lose things do we? Whether it's an elderly loved one, a favourite CD or a five pound note. I didn't know what made me keep persevering. I think it was because we were so different but so much alike. But I had got used to the little things he used to say. He would text late at night ordering me to bring Sterling Superkings cigarettes and Smirnoff vodka. Then when I'd get there he'd tell me to pour myself a drink. Then, when I only poured a small one he would stare at me and say, "Don't embarrass yourself girl!" He'd go the toilet and tell me not to go at all that night, never mind "leave it ten minutes," or he tell me not to nick the toilet rolls. I had grown used to being offended; being called Vanessa Feltz and a blue cunt as I was a City fan. I didn't know why but I didn't want to lose that.

A friendship had developed where we could tell each other things. Well, he would tell me and I would listen and I would tell him things and he would yawn and inform me it was time to leave as I had passed his boredom threshold. Why did I put up with it I hear you ask. I'll tell you why because he had become my mate. My mate, Williams.

At times I admired and respected him and other times I hated him. Hated the fact he seen me as a man, hated the fact he never listened and just talked, incessantly. I hated the fact he was a red. I hated the fact that I could have stood in front of him stark bollock naked and he would have told me to shift my arse so he could watch Rita and Norris talking about who was going to fill up the sherbet dip jar in Corrie. But the night I left (well I didn't leave; I was ejected like a pissed up teenager from a night club who'd just been sick all over the bar), I knew I had been in the wrong; so all the hard work was up to me. And all I'll say is that it was hard but it brought me the reward of having one of the best mates you'd ever what. We all want and need one don't we? Are you jealous yet, reader?

So after two very long weeks of wondering why, for the first time in my life, someone hated me, we were friends again. I remembered my ex-husband must have hated me a bit because he had tried to run me off the A580 and kill me but that hadn't offended me at all. I wondered why I was so bothered about Williams hating me. I'd only known him about a month. Really, I shouldn't have gave a proverbial shit. I was confused. So I won't go into the details of how it was repaired but I'll just say that it was gradual; just like it should be. Anyway, to be friends again just before Christmas was the best present I could have wished for. Well, actually I got a better one. It had zips and was made of leather but more of that later! And no, it's not what you think, you dirty gits. So ladies, I'll just say the deed was done.

I knew it was just sex for him. The thing that give it away was the fact that 2.5 seconds later he jumped up ran off quicker than Usain Bolt after a dodgy pint of Holt's Regal and a Vindaloo and asked did I want anything from the shop. Yea, I thought. A fuckin' black marker pen so you can write "Idiot" on my forehead. But I just replied, "Yea, Maltesers please," hanging on to the last bit of dignity I had.

A thought flashed through my mind that he had a hidden camera and he was going to sell it some dodgy video shop on Bolton Road. However, common sense made me realise he wouldn't get much more than two pound fifty for it (If he was lucky). In fact he'd probably have to pay them. Feeling a complete idiot and hurt, I lay there quietly. Having learnt very quickly never to believe a word that comes out of a man's mouth ever again, I went downstairs and tried to push it out of my head. I knew he had done. But not for the same reasons. I don't need to say anymore do I ladies?

Men, I'll just try and make an analogy out of this episode for you all. Imagine you are carrying two big heavy bags of shopping. It's irrelevant where the shopping is from. But it's heavy. Got that in your heads? Hard I know to picture this scenario. Shopping bags are the things you put the weekly shop in. They vary in price, some you have to pay for, others are free. They have handles and are usually carried by women. However picture you have been carrying these two bags for weeks. You've walked about 20 miles and suddenly you want, no you need, to put them down. But you can't; someone has to carry them for you because there's something that could easily spill inside them. There's a passer-by so you ask them to carry the bags for a minute for you. You're not bothered who the passer-by is as long as they carry the bags and offload the weight to relieve you for a minute. Get the picture now? Enough said? Let's move on then ....and quickly.

Some weeks later Williams asked me to pick up a prescription for quit smoking patches. More chance of me getting stuck alone in a lift with Daniel Craig for two hours and needing to go to Hope's A & E department afterwards with severe exhaustion than him giving up, I thought. However as usual I said: "No problem, mate." I went to the hairdressers first after he told me there was no rush to get them. One o'clock was fine.

It had taken me years to find a hairdresser that wasn't too dear and pretentious but I had found one and enjoyed the natter and the brew. I soon began to relax in the company of unpretentious women talking about things that mattered. My phone rang and because of the noise of the dryers I put the speaker facility on.

"Shazza, where the fuck are you with my patches?" he asked.

"Be about two, running late. Just having my hair cut," I shouted above the noise.

"You having a Brazilian, mate?" he enquired.

At the precise moment he asked me the dryer went silent, as did the other women in the salon. His question could be heard by everyone in there, including a woman who looked puzzled and no doubt wondered if there was a room at the back of the salon where you could get down and be intimate with men from more far afield than Ordsall.

"Bastard," I said.

"Tell him I'm not insured for 'owt like that. Got sued once but I won't go into that!" my hairdresser said.

I cut him off. The first time I'd ever done that. He did it all the time. I felt myself go red and then suddenly burst out laughing and informed the rest of the women there that the caller was okay really. Just a little bit.....well thoughtless sometimes. Didn't think before he put his mouth in gear. Or so I thought...... because that afternoon was going to change that perception forever. Well, for a couple of hours anyway.

I arrived at his and he told me that his mate was picking him up for a drink. It was a bloke called Trotty. I had gone to Primary school with Trotty but Williams had been his friend for over 30 years. Why Trotty hadn't been awarded an MBE for these services to charity I didn't know. I knew the friendship was a good one and was happy for Williams that he was going to have a good afternoon with his mate.

Trotty mentioned to Williams that his wife didn't know he was going out for a swift one.

I remember wondering if he had just forgotten to tell her or he was just a twat.

Williams then proceeded to tell Trotty that I had been doing his cleaning and ironing free of charge. Trotty asked did he make me wear a French maid's outfit to which Williams' replied: "Oh yea, mate, she does a lot of bending over when she cleans that fireplace I can tell you!"

"Bastard!" I thought again. This was a word that I was beginning to use on a regular basis where Williams was involved. He told me he would always be discreet about "the deed." Discreet my arse! Anyway, I offered to drop them off so it would save them taxi fare.

Not one to look a gift horse in the mouth Williams said: "Yea, go on then. You can pick a few of my mates up as well seeing though you're offering. It won't take you long."

As we drove down the top road Williams offered to fix my car heater (I'm still waiting readers). I think hell will freeze over first or Accrington Stanley will sign a top striker for £26 million (getting the picture?).

We passed Salford landmarks and spoke about what the city had lost: the Carlton cinema, several schools and how great pubs had been converted into Indian restaurants and even churches. The drive went quickly as we talked about all the places we had grown up with. After telling us about how he had nicked lead of Seedley Baths' roof when he was just a kid, Williams then told us about his quest to find out about the museum in Buile Hill Park and who it belonged to now. He told us about his rubbing shoulders with a local MP and how he had received an official note headed letter from The House of Commons. I wondered if he could have hidden depths and be some sort of maverick for the people of Salford.

I picked up his friends: Nick and his son Saul. After chatting briefly to Nick I was pleasantly surprised that Williams knew normal people. It passed my mind how on earth did they put up with him.

"Come in for a quick one," he said.

"Oh, I don't drink in the day", I said, which was partly true. I didn't drink much in the day I should have said.

"Go on," Trotty encouraged me.

I waivered for about a second and said: "Oh, go on then. I'll have one," I replied. Four double Bacardi and cokes later and I was starting to feel warm inside. This warmth was not entirely due to the drink; it was more to do with what was coming out of Williams' mouth. And for once it wasn't bullshit. There was a rapport between the four men that made a refreshing change from listening to conversations about hysterectomies and Emmerdale. I spoke to Nick, who I learnt was Williams' cousin. His cousin and I spoke at length about various things. We discovered we both had similar childhood experiences and how we had both grown up doubting our abilities. But as I spoke to Nick it was obvious that the relationship between him and Williams was more than that of cousins. They both took great pride in the fact that they were what they called "Salford Irish" meaning that their grandparents had come over from Ireland to help build the Manchester Ship Canal. Nick knew Williams inside out. He knew that he was erratic, unpredictable, capable of getting into trouble, didn't think things through but, and it's a big but, he was a deep, caring and intelligent man who sometimes lost his way. Nick was more of a brother to Williams; that was clear.

As Williams stood outside having his tenth ciggy of the day with Saul, Nick told me about how when Williams' dad was dying he had asked Nick to look after Williams. Nick said that he had tried his best and would continue to do so. And do you know what? I believe he will.

Williams asked (no told) me to take a picture of him and Trotty. I took the picture of them both grinning after their fourth pint and Williams said: "Put it on Facebook, mate!"

"Nah, don't do that. My missus will see it won't she?" said Trotty, sounding like a man feared for his life. Shithouse.

Saul, Williams' nephew, was telling him about being in a band; a rock band. Williams asked him: "Do you want your Uncle Knobhead to write you some lyrics for the band?"

Oh, dear God! I thought. What the fuck is he gonna come up with? I asked myself.

Saul, a polite and genuine young man smiled and said: "Ok, then". Williams and Saul locked heads and the rest of us waited for the results.

Williams decided because Christmas was coming up he would write a Christmas song as they're the ones that "make the money. Look at that bastard Noddy Holder", he said."They bring him out every Christmas, the Brummy bastard" he added eloquently. Anyway, after having his head down for five minutes he came up with the following: I'm dreaming of a white Christmas It's not the one you're thinking about It's a bag of powder to deaden the pain Where the dealer is the only one who gains People rushing all excited Credit cards bashed, Visa delighted Jingle bells all a ringing Wonder why my head is binging Coming down isn't much fun Like looking down a loaded gun. Pull the trigger, get me out is this what Christmas is all about? The only turkey I will see is the cold shivering wreck that's me Merry Christmas, one and all Time is up, I've had my fall (Copyright to this song owned by Simon Williams: any attempts to copy or use without permission will result in legal action) Well, we were pleasantly surprised I can tell you.

He told Saul that if he and his band couldn't make something of that then they needed their arses kicking. We were shocked that he could produce something so poignant so quickly and sat there in stunned silence.

Williams looked at his nephew and asked him: "Who's Uncle Knobhead now, eh?"

I think Saul was as surprised as I was. He looked at his Uncle Knobhead and smiled. He didn't need to say anything as the smile said everything, it said "thank you" and "I think you're great", all at the same time. All of a sudden Williams' phone binged with a Face book notification. He looked at the message that had come through and smiled. It was from an old school friend, Jackie Hobbart, who had put 'pair of old buddies.' We all smiled.

Two seconds later it binged again. Trotty didn't smile as he seen it was his wife who had added the newest comment which read 'pair of wankers, more like.' Williams laughed loudly. Trotty, however, did not. "Get to the bar, Trotty, you tight git and make sure you get Shazza a double and don't embarrass yourself !" Williams said.

Trotty came back from the bar with several drinks and Williams took mine from him , smelled it and said: " Smells a bit Cokey, mate!" he said.

Williams' phone binged yet again and when he looked at the screen and read the next message. His face lit up like a Christmas tree as he noticed a 'like.'

"What you smiling at, Williams?" asked Trotty.

"I've got a like from Rose Stubbs", he replied.

"You've got to let it go, mate", said Williams' uncle. The

men talked about how he had liked Rose since school and how he would not let go the idea of getting her. He had liked her since primary school and had always liked her. He would carry on wanting her until he either popped his clogs or he did actually get her.

I listened to the group of men trying to tell him he was never going to get anywhere with her but he was undeterred. He was like a teenager but in a way I wanted to help him. Part of me didn't want to and part of me did.

After drinking my eighth Bacardi I decided it was time to go as I was going out later, so I said bye to everyone knowing they were going to have a great time. If I ask you, dear readers, have you ever told a little white lie? What would you say? 100% of you would say yes. So I will tell you what happened at the close of play that night. Williams rang about eleven o'clock. I was at a doo with a friend with every intention of calling at Williams' for a swift vodka later on. If I said he sounded paralytic that would be an understatement.

"Come and pick me up mate, I'm in Eccles and I'm wankered." he said.

"Get a taxi, you tight git!" I told him.

"Please Shazza, I want to talk to you", he slurred.

"What about? The fact City are gonna take the title again?" I asked.

"Listen mate", he said, sounding as though he was going to pass out at any minute. "My mates said I could do a lot worse than you. A lot worse in fact. So I think you better come and we'll have a talk. My mates like you, our Nicole likes you. So I might as well like you" he finished.

The last sentence was the equivalent of Eric Cantona being told he was average but United might as well sign him because they had a few bob spare and room on the books for another player. Yes, ladies. You're thinking the same aren't you? Well you're right and yes, I had never felt so insulted in decades. Not since someone in The Silver Screen told me I looked like a cross between Peter O'Toole and Victoria Wood (yes, I did tell them to "Fuck off!"). So you know what I'm going to say don't you? And you'd be right. I told a little white lie. I told him I had been sick and that I couldn't possibly pick him up and was too ill to go to his and then I promptly said goodnight. I reckoned it would save the embarrassment of getting there and him being asleep or worse still not even remembering what he'd said.

Some lies are justified aren't they? And as sure as eggs are egg he didn't remember. But what I remembered more than being insulted was the respect that young man shown to his Uncle. I remembered the friendship I could see in front of me around that table that afternoon. And I remembered how Williams taught me to never to judge a book by its cover. Good thing I lied really. I had made up my mind that I was not going to be made a fool off and wasn't going to be anybody's second best.

Chapter 6-Christmas

As Christmas approached I remember Williams asking me when was the normal time to put a tree up. He asked me how much it would cost for a tree, decorations and lights.

When I told him it would be about fifty quid he said: "Oh, I don't think so ! I know where's there's a tree," in a voice that was on a mission. He said he didn't want his kids to be disappointed and somehow I knew they wasn't going to be.

When I went the next time, there was a tree touching the ceiling decorated with baubles and lights. I asked where he had got the tree from: "Was it Tesco or Home and Bargain?"

"No PLD, mate", he said. And then he went on to tell me the story....... "Well, I couldn't see my own kids disappointed could I ?" he said. "I'd seen this box lying about at work with the words Christmas tree 8 feet on it and I thought my kids would love that!. It was like father Christmas had left me a pressie early. If they had put it up a bit earlier they might still have it! Serves 'em right. Them bastards have got more money than I have!", he said indignantly. "It took three of us an hour each to nick it. One lad Binnsy was talking to the gaffer keeping him distracted. Young Azza was keeping dogout and I was up in the office getting it. I got it and walked passed them as bold as brass thinking that my kids were gonna be happy! And the best of it is, it'll keep them quiet on Saturday for four hours putting the bugger up. I think I'll have a few vodies and we'll sing some carols. Sorted, mate!" he said and smiled to himself at his sheer cheek.

A few days later he texted asking me could I go round and wrap some presents as that was "woman's work and you like doing stuff like that don't you?" Sexist bastard I thought, Wrap your own fuckin' presents. But when he added that there was one for me I put my foot down and hit about 67 mph down Bolton Road. I wasn't materialistic but I was going to get something out of the bastard if it killed me. Probably a box of After Eight from Poundland, Tight arse.

When I got there he had had a few and he chucked the Sellotape and wrapping paper at me and said: " Well hurry up then, there's loads of 'em!".

I started to wrap them and did a neat job if I say so myself. I wrapped toys and an expensive jumper for his son-in-law who he said better appreciate it or else. I wrapped his grandson's present and he said he hoped the 'littl' 'un' liked it. It was clear to me that he loved the bones of all the kids in his family and I smiled as I began wrapping the last present, which was a beautiful brown Prada bag. It was really classy and the leather smelt lovely. I said: "Oh, your Amanda will love that, mate" I wrapped them all and he gave me a vodka to say thank you and after drinking it, I left.

A week later I got a text telling me he had got me a special present and I better come round and get it and bring some ciggies as well. I got there and he promptly went into the kitchen and returned with an ironing board.

"There you are, mate. Thought you might like it. Do you want to put it up and try it out? There's a pile there you can have a go with", he said.

I couldn't believe it. How thoughtful. An ironing board. Then he added: "You got to understand my mam's seventy now, It's not fair asking her to do it. Oh, and be careful 'cos some of that gear cost me a lot of money. Designer labels there, mate. Cost me a fuckin fortune."

After I finished the pile Williams said: " No, I'm only joking mate, there's your real one," he said as he passed me a plastic carrier from Tesco.

"I haven't wrapped it, cos basically I couldn't be arsed. You don't mind do you? It's the thought that counts," he added.

I opened the bag and there, inside, was a Mulberry leather bag. Nice as well. I was shocked I can tell you. I thought it was a wind up at first and the bastard was going to take it off me. Just the sort of thing he'd do. But no. It was mine. Chuffed was not the word.

He said: "I thought you might need one; smarten your appearance up a bit, mate!"

I knew it was well meant and said "thank you". Williams, for once, had not embarrassed himself. Christmas came and went and then a new year came...........

Chapter 7- A New Year

His parting words to me on New Year's Eve, after he used the leftover fireworks from his birthday and emptied a litre bottle of Smirnoff, were: "All the best, mate."

I went straight to bed because I hate New Year's Eve and

wanted to be asleep by twelve. But I couldn't sleep so I decided to have a look on Face book and see what friends were up to as the midnight hour approached. As I looked at the news feed for recent activity I noticed Williams' name and his comments rolling up the screen. Williams had told me he had been going on Face book quite a lot recently as it was a way of communicating with Rose Stubbs. He had told me that she was playing him like a violin but he felt he had to keep trying as he knew that eventually he would get through to her and she would see that he was a good 'un.

He had put loads of comments on that were obviously aimed at Rose and he wanted her to read them. He had already told her that there was someone he would look after and care for if she gave him the chance and after that his cryptic messages were getting a bit beyond a joke. Messages like: Good things come to those who wait. While you are single, your pocket will jingle Save the best 'til last You're just too good to be true I would rather be single and lonely, than be in a relationship and unhappy. I had seen these messages appear over the weeks and thought he must have either been a bit merry or he must have been making a concerted effort to catch her attention. But I noticed his little ploy was not working because the only attention he was getting in the form of replies, was from his ex-wives' sisters (probably laughing), Jackie Hobbart (who always encouraged him with sincere comments) and Maureen Hedgehog, an old school friend. Williams told me the day he took advice off them would be the day he captained United (the other love of his live).

Every now and again, Rose would give him a little ray of hope that he was not wasting his time. She would send him messages asking how he was (she was probably just being friendly but he took it as a positive sign which encouraged him even more). It had all started when, as a five year old child their eyes met across Langworthy Road school playground. To him, she was his English rose. And he had never let it go. How would anyone be able to compete with that?

Chapter 8- Williams' workmates

Williams always seemed happy when he was telling me about work. If ever a job was made for a person, it was this one. He always professed to be busy and hard at it. However the proof was in the pudding and I KNEW he did fuck all for most of the day. He would send pointless texts or stupid jokes or tell me what was on his butties. He told me he worked so hard that as soon as he got in from work he would fall asleep from exhaustion. I knew all he did all day was have a good crack with his mates and the only time they worked was in the last two hours getting ready to pack up.

Williams was in charge of his little gang, which consisted of Binnsy, an inbred from Farnworth, who loved snooker and his missus Diane. Williams told me that Binnsy had shed loads of grandkids and that he was forever buying prams for his family's new arrivals. Then, there was young Azza, a quiet lad who had joined as a junior straight from school. Williams said he was the sort of lad you'd want your daughter to bring home. He had two pastimes: the gym and chillin'.

Williams obviously cared for these lads. That was clear in the way he told me about what had happened in the course of the day. They were little stories about the gang's mishaps, scrapes and generally their ability to do nothing all day. One night Williams was telling me about the day the gang was working in Moss Side. He was reversing a seven and half ton truck into a non-existent gap. It had taken him thirty minutes to manoeuvre the truck into the gap as there was only a two centimetre space either side. He told me he had been buzzing at his achievement because getting the truck so near to the job had saved the gang time (and effort) to offload the slates onto the back of the vehicle. He said the gang worked hard to try and get an early flit and they had filled the back of the truck quickly with the slates. However when Williams had come to reverse the truck out of the space he had forget to open out the wing mirrors that he had previously folded in. Well, he said he forgot, personally I think he just couldn't be arsed getting out of the truck once he had sat down.

Anyway the reason is irrelevant; it is what happened next that is important. Williams told me he put his foot on the pedal and a split second later he heard, to his horror, a loud crunching sound. He had reversed the truck (a seven and half tonner don't forget, loaded with about four ton of slates!) into the back of a brand new Mercedes Benz people carrier. Now I know not a lot bothers Williams. He is unaffected by most things. But this was a faux pas of epic proportion. He walked down the path of the house where the car was parked to explain his actions to its owner. He knocked on the door. The door was opened by a 6ft 6inch black man who Williams described as a "dead ringer for Lennox Lewis, a pumped up Lennox Lewis I hasten to add!"

He took great pleasure in retelling me the conversation: "Look mate, I've just reversed my truck into your car and it's a fuckin' right off!" he said.

"What happen now?" the man asked.

Williams said he was obviously not a native of Moss Side. "My insurance gets in touch with your insurance and they speak to each other and my insurance pays you out" Williams said calmly.

"I'm not insured", the man replied, obviously unaware of the implications' of what he had just said.

"Really?" said Williams. "Shall I phone the police or do you want to do it?" he added. Williams walked off and told the rest of the gang his good news.

Binnsy said to Williams:" If you were on a plane and it

crashed, you would land in the sea, you stuffy bastard."

They drove off in the truck, which funnily enough didn't have a mark on it, laughing about his ability to walk away from it without a care in the world.

Another story was the day the gang was working on a site in Wythenshawe. Williams said he couldn't trust the site manager to run a bath let alone a site. Williams, the cocky clever bastard that he is, took an instant dislike to the manager. But as Williams told me once it's not what other people think about you, it's what you think about yourself that matters. Williams had every faith in his gang that they would do the best job possible at the site. Williams told me he had a massive argument with the site manager and he was fuming. He told me that as he drove off the site the manager was still "mouthing it" to him from the other side of the road. Well, Williams decided at this point to drive the truck, mount the pavement and pin his manager against some bushes. Williams said the bumper of the truck was a millimetre away from the gaffer's nose. I think you and me would call it "ramming" someone to within an inch of their life. He then proceeded to tell the site manager: "You're not so fuckin' clever now are you mate?"

Well after this little "encounter" there was an emergency meeting back at the office. Williams had received a phone call to get his arse in there as he was in deep shit..... Again! The meeting was in the Board room and before he went in, Williams was informed that what was about to happen, or anything that was about to be said, was "off the record".

The meeting started with the "big" boss, Harry Worthington, saying: "We have been told that there was, for want of a better word, an incident today. The site manager has told us that you are nothing but a big bully and you were aggressive towards him."

Williams considered the accusation and replied with these carefully chosen words: "I work in the building trade; not at the

Bolshoi fuckin ballet!" He then pointed at the accuser and said: "Are you accusing me of bullying?"

"No", replied the site manager.

"Well it must be you then who's accusing me!" he said to Harry Worthington.

To which the boss replied: "Well, you do come over as being very aggressive."

"Yea, but that doesn't make me a bully! " Williams replied.

Peter Adams, from the company's main office and was there as a neutral observer, stood there in disbelief. After what Williams described as ' a bit of toin' and throwin' that was the end of that.

Another close shave. Williams told me about another friend, Benny Jarvis, who had joined the gang before Binnsy. He spoke affectionately about this younger man and I think Williams liked him because the lad was as daft as a brush too. However, this lad must have suffered in silence and Williams was to hear tragic news about this likeable lad. It knocked Williams for six. It bothered him because, as everyone who has experienced it, he felt the lad should have told him something was wrong. And if he had things would have been different. But sadly, we cannot reverse time can we? We have to deal with things as they happen. Williams told me that everyone has bad cards dealt to them but it's how you play them that matter. Silly, trivial things didn't seem so important to Williams anymore after hearing the news that this young man had taken his own life.

Williams reflected on his own life and immediately deleted his Face book account. He said that if anyone needed to contact him, then they knew his number or they knew where to find him. What he learnt that night was that he never wanted this to happen again to any of his friends and all he wanted was that if anyone was suffering in silence like Benny, they should know that all they had to do was talk to him. Williams told me he was very lucky. He could count his good friends on more than one hand. They say that don't they? That you can count your true friends on one hand. Those that will believe in you regardless of what you've done. It was two days later he received a text from Rose saying that she was thinking of him at this sad time...........

Chapter 9- The End?

Well, things moved on for my mate Williams. Texts from Rose, that had started off being polite enquiries about how he was doing, gradually turned into much more and very quickly, lengthy conversations grew into deep and meaningful exchanges of mutual feelings between the pair of them. I had tried over the months to clean his house, get his ironing under control (I drew the line at cleaning his toilet and pressing his boxers) and generally get him ready for taking Rose back to his abode. As I look back on how our friendship had grew, I smiled.

The first few weeks had been a case of getting to know each other, followed by learning about each other's views and opinions and what made them laugh. Well, I had to listen to his point of view then he would just watch TV while I told him mine. But we made each other laugh. It was the ability to throw sarcasm at each other that made us laugh. I had learnt that his morals were rock solid and he taught me so many things. He told me that I had taught him things and that was enough reward for me.

I had been torn between hating him and wanting him as more than a friend. But as the weeks progressed I realised that was never going to happen and I could never compete with his English rose. I had realised that he could never give me what I wanted or needed. I wanted someone who made me laugh but cared about me as more than a mate. Someone who came up behind me when I washed the pots and grabbed me, turned me round, put his hands through my hair and masterfully kissed me until I passed out! Then when I came round he would drag me upstairs and ....and.........Readers, just what sort of book do you think this is? Well it isn't Fifty Shades of Grey that's for sure. I wanted someone who knew if I was happy, sad or worried. Someone who wanted to share the good things in life.....like KFC, Blackpool lights or a day under the quilt watching TV. And anyway Williams didn't regard me like that. He was my mate. And that is a very privileged position to be in.

So, picture this. His house is sorted; there is no longer two inches of burnt toast on the worktops. Everywhere is spotless. Well actually, readers, I'm lying. I only did it once and realised it was a waste of time. I might be thoughtful and caring but I ain't flogging a dead horse for no one. Williams had changed but thankfully not completely. He hadn't lost what made him unique. The humour, the caring side that he tries to hide and only shows to those in his inner circle and his ability to tell tall stories were all still there. But he had began to think about things more; especially the things that had potential to be taken the wrong way by people. He was still scathing to people that deserved it but still made everyone around him happy. In fact, Williams was beginning to question his assumption that he had always thought that Rose was out of his league. Maybe, just maybe, he thought, she was out his league. Now, at long last, Williams realised no one was out of his league. But things happened quickly.

It was a week to the next six monthly school reunion and I had said I would go.

I asked Williams was he going and he said: "No, mate. I've had a text from Rose and she's said "Yes." So will you iron me that Ralph Lauren polo for me mate?"

"What's the magic word, mate?", I asked him. He ignored me and just said: "Just do a good job, mate".

"No, don't wear that mate. That checked shirt is better, show your physique off better!" I replied. It didn't. I had burnt a big fuck off hole in his Ralph Lauren and had rolled it up and hid it behind his wardrobe. I wasn't going fork out £150 for a new one I can tell you. I wished him luck and hugged him. I knew it was going to be a success. And do you know why? Because he deserved it to be. So, as he got ready, I went home to get changed for the reunion.

This time it didn't have the same appeal as the last one. The last one was where I had met my mate and no-one would ever be a mate like he had been to me. But never the less I set off. I had decided to drive and stay sober as I wanted to maintain a certain classy air about me this time and not appear like a younger version of Vinegar Vera. As I was getting ready Williams was driving to meet Rose. This was the moment he had waited over forty years for. He didn't tell me the details of what happened that night. I had to read about it the week later.

He had been driving along a road and hit a patch of black ice. His BMW had served and gone headlong into a lamp post. The car was squashed up like a concertina. Or so the Salford City Reporter said. There's not many people who get themselves into the Reporter twice in six months is there? And on the front page too. Anyway, the sirens of the ambulance didn't wake him as he was drifting between this world and the next.

I had just started to park my car in town when my phone rang. I didn't recognise the whole number but I instantly recognised it as a Salford number. The voice said: "Hello, this is Salford Royal Hospital. I'm Nurse Brown. We've a man admitted into A & E and your number is the last one he rung. Could you possibly come down and help us identify the man please?" I asked was the man in the morgue. The nurse informed me that he wasn't dead but he was in a bad way and could I get there as soon as possible. There was only one person it could be.

Williams had only rang me about an hour before just to say that he had found the Ralph Lauren behind his wardrobe and he wanted a ton off me to get a new one. Cheeky bastard. That's the thanks you get. I started the engine and drove as fast as I could to the hospital so that I could get there in time to say goodbye to my friend. I ran through the corridors of the hospital to the A &

E department and asked a nurse to take me to the room where Williams was. The nurse knew him from a previous stay after he had received an injury from a firearm. He told his kids and me it was a bullet from an elephant gun when he was in the Congo jungle. As tall stories go it was one of the less believable.

I went in the room and there he was lying on the bed. He was wired up like the Six Million Dollar man. He had a saline drip inserted into his arm. Readers, I'm not ashamed to say that I had tears running down my face. I cannot tell you how I felt because I was numb. I was going to lose my newly found friend. He had been on the way to meet the love of his life and the chance had been snatched away from him. I leaned over and patted his chest (the one chiselled from Salford's finest marble) and, as I whispered my last goodbye, I knew it was serious. I asked the nurse did she think he would pull through. She didn't answer me but simply put her hand on my shoulder. I was gutted. There had been times when I hated him. I could have murdered him. Quite easily. But I would have hated to see anything happen to him.

I left the room and walked slowly down the corridor into the cold air outside. I sat in the car, put the seat belt on and switched on the radio to try and take my mind off losing my mate. I should have stayed to wait for the flat line to appear on the medical screen above his bed or until I could no longer hear the beeping sounds which signified the end of his life; but I couldn't. I couldn't stay and see him fade away quietly from this world. He lived life every day with a energy that I admired. I didn't want to see my mate go gently up that escalator to heaven. I thought that if he was going to die he would go in a blaze of glory; just like all the good ones did. I turned the engine on. The man on the radio had just finished reading the news. The usual war zone reports and other shocking events from around the world. But it was all insignificant. Then he introduced the next song: "And next we have The Stone Rose....s..... with

Resurrection", he said. At that point I knew he was going to be ok. All didn't seem lost. There was a glimmer....a light that never went out. His mate Binnsy was right. If he had been in a plane he would have landed in the sea and swam to the shore. I knew. I just knew.

Chapter 10 -Resurrection

I went to the hospital every day. In the week I went at night for the evening visiting hours and at weekends I went in the day. This routine lasted for a month. There were days when I arrived at the door of his private room and looked at him lying on the bed; his face was so ashen that I thought he had gone to meet his maker. I made friends with the nurses who looked after him. Well, they came and checked him regularly and did all they could. A couple of them remembered him from his last stay a few years before.

I asked one nurse, Philomena, if he had been a good patient. I couldn't for one moment believe he was but she answered me with an honesty that could only come from a woman who had clearly been tested beyond her patience.

"Well, let's put it this way, my dear", she said. "I've worked here for nearly twenty five years and I've never had to nurse anyone so feckin' cheeky, I can tell you", she added. She rolled her eyes towards the ceiling and said: "Can I have some more soup, love? Can I have a brew, love? Have you got just a little bit of pepper to go on my spuds? Have you got a couple of extra pillows, nurse? That toast was nice, nurse, could just eat the same again, any chance? " she rattled off his requests and I got the distinct impression that she was giving me the answer to my question in a polite a way as possible.

"Did you always give him what he wanted?" I asked.

"Oh, Jesus, no!" she said. "I drew the line at fish, chips, mushy peas and a barm from The Battered Cod. Oh, and young Nurse Jody Hookway said no to his request to being rubbed down with Johnson's baby oil to ease his aching muscle," she informed me.

That sounded like the Williams I knew. If you gave him an inch he would take a mile. But this time they had not been bombarded with requests for extra servings of jam roly poly and custard or another six rounds of toast. This time he lay silent and still with only the regular beep of the monitor that stood like a guard at the side of his bed.

His children went and tried to tell him about their days; about what they had done at school and at the weekends.

I went when it was quiet and sat and watched the screen for signs of a flicker or looked at his face to see if his eyes twitched. I made up things to see if he would wake up. I'd tell him Rose was visiting him that night or I'd tell him Cantona had heard about him being in a coma and he was going to fly in from Paris and bring him a signed shirt. I even told him Morrissey had sent him a get well card. Nothing worked. So I just read the football reports from the daily papers. Made them up half the time just to make them more exciting. I told him what the nurses had said about the fact they had needed to import a special urine bottle for him because the ones they had were too small. That it had arrived from Taiwan by courier in a box labelled "Contents: Urine bottle python size". I hated making things up but I thought my words would reach his ego that had been lying dormant for nearly a month now. But again nothing.

I didn't know whether to stop going and just wait for the hospital to ring me one day and tell me that he'd either woken up and faded away. His eldest daughter held on to the hope he would wake up and start moaning for a brew and a cig. She had told me she wanted him to see his new grandchild who was due to be born any day. I wasn't so sure he would. Part of me didn't want him to because he had been the perfect man whilst he was in the coma. He listened (or appeared to be) without constantly interrupting. He couldn't call me Vanessa Feltz or criticise my driving or cooking. It was perfect ....only he wasn't making me laugh. He wasn't making anyone else laugh either. And that was a huge part of him.

I sat on the plastic visitor's chair and looked at his face. I wondered whether he could hear anything that was going on around him. Did he know how long he had been there? Was he too cold? Was he too warm? Did he know City had regained the title? He fuckin' would do as soon as he woke up. That was my first priority; to make the bastard suffer. Suffer like he had made me suffer watching him lying there motionless night after night; week after week. One Sunday evening I was sat at his bedside when I noticed, for the first time, his face looked peaceful. The crevices around his eyes had disappeared and he almost (I repeat, almost) looked handsome.

It reminded me of a day when I had asked him did he regard himself as being good looking. He had replied: "Am I handsome? Am I handsome?" He pointed at himself and added, "This ain't no fuckin' accident, mate!" I had laughed at the time. I would have done anything for him to wake up now and say that. I got up to leave and went over to the bed. I patted his hand and started to walk away when suddenly my phone started to ring. I recognised the number as being Williams' daughter, Amanda.

But it was the voice was a man who said: "Hello, is that Sharon?"

"Yes, it is. Who's that?" I asked.

"It's Amanda's partner, Gary. Amanda asked me to ring you and let you know we are the proud parents of a baby daughter," the voice said.

After saying congratulations and thanks for letting me know, I went and sat down next to Williams' bed. I shook him gently and said: "Listen, mate, you're a granddad to a little girl." I was just about to plead with him to wake up when suddenly I seen the smallest twitch of his eyelid.

Slowly he opened his eyes and I suddenly remembered just how blue his eyes were. I was never sure if it was cataracts or he had the best eyes since Paul Newman. It didn't matter anyway. He was awake.

He opened his mouth and very faintly said: " What time is it? Am I late for work?"

My mate was back for good.

Chapter 11- An out of body experience

It was as though he had been to work the day before and just woken up to another day. Another long, laborious day at work. Well, I say work, but in fact I think Williams only worked for about 10% of his working day; the rest was spent drinking tea, going to the nearest chippy and putting bets on.

He looked slowly around the room and noticed the monitor, his name above the bed and the get well cards on the little bedside cabinet.

I went to get a nurse who looked slightly disappointed (no, actually gutted is a more accurate word) at the news my mate had woken up. I think she must have been one of the staff who had attended him during his stay there the year before. I felt sorry for him. He looked disorientated and puzzled as to why he was there. I thought about how the fact that he had found himself in clean pyjamas lying underneath clean, white sheets must have been a shock in itself.

I looked at him, smiled and asked him did he know what had happened?

He said he vaguely remembered about the crash and how he had been on his way to meet Rose, but that was all.

I told him about how he had been in a coma for just over a month. I told him I'd been every day and how all his family knew he was going to be alright. I told him City had won the Premiership and that Rose had got married to a vet two weeks after he had failed to meet her.

"Oh, I was a bit worried she might still be waiting at the restaurant", he said on hearing the news. He looked a little groggy and added: " ou'll never believe what's happened to me, mate, seriously!"

"What?" I asked him, dreading to hear what was coming next. He'd been in a coma for a month; how much trouble could he cause? With Williams though, anything was possible. The nurse had informed me not to stay long as he would be tired and any stress, physical exertion or excitement would be detrimental to his recovery. "Excitement! Physical exertion!" I said, "They'll be no chance of that, Nurse", I assured her. Williams' idea of excitement was getting a full litre bottle of Smirnoff for less than fourteen quid from Tesco or getting an accumulator up at BetFred's on a Saturday afternoon.

"Seriously, you're not going to believe me. I think I had an out of body experience. I went to heaven and they've sent me back down 'cos I wasn't ready to go yet", he told me. He had the most sincere expression on his face that I had ever seen. "Shazza, I've been up there, honestly! I got to St Peter's gates and everyone was there to meet me", he said, unaware of how absurd his story sounded.

However, I listened knowing that this was not going to take a couple of minutes and the nurse would be livid at me for staying. I asked him: " Who was there waiting for you, mate?"

"Me Granny Costigan was there. Stood there waiting for me, she was. She's been up there since the 70s but I used to remember her as clear as anything when I was a kid. She used to say she had a three pound note and give me a pound one" he told me."I could always tell she was Irish even before the jokes started coming out about the Irish. It felt like only days since I had last seen her". "And me Granddad Costigan was there waiting. I could see he couldn't wait to speak to me. The first thing he said was "I told you we'd win the league eventually". He'd been a blue and said they would win it one day."

Now, let me just tell you that Williams can spin a yarn, tell a tale, exaggerate or bullshit with the best of them. I knew that and half the time I used to humour him because I knew he was only doing it to make people have a good laugh. Yet, this time his face was deadly serious and everything he said was in total earnest. I truly believed that he thought he had been up there. Who was I to dispute him?

"Shazza, you'll never believe who came to see me! Just have a guess."

"Er, John Lennon?"

"Nah, have another guess", he prompted me.

At this point I wished I was in a coma because I knew it was going to be a very long story. "Er, Elvis and Frank Sinatra riding pillion on the back of James Dean's motorbike?" I said.

"Nah, you're taking the piss now, mate. This is serious. I'll tell you who. Georgie fuckin' Best that's who, mate. Besty. And he only wanted me to join his team; Heaven's Eleven", he exclaimed. "It was mad, mate. There was a massive bright white light, attracting me to these big iron gates. There was a bloke stood there with a big white Jewish beard holding a clipboard and a school register. I told him my name and he said it's not your turn yet and if your name's not down on here you're not coming in. Then they put me on the return escalator. The really weird bit is that I seen my Dad and Benny Jarvis but I couldn't talk to them as it wasn't my turn. I wasn't allowed but I waved and they waved back. I was happy though, mate, because at least I knew that they had got to heaven. Then I heard a voice saying that Amanda had given birth and I thought, "Fuck me, my alarm's not gone off again, and I realised I must have been dreaming. I woke up and thought what's all this attention? What's all these Get Well cards? God, that fruit looks a bit dusty. Then I suddenly remembered the crash. I remember skidding on the road and heading for the lamp post and......Oh, mate.....thank God I'm still here. I've got another forty years left yet. I seen my sell by date on that clipboard."

He fell asleep shortly after finishing the story. The nurses told me, that all being well, he could leave at the end of that week. To be honest I think they just wanted to get rid of him.

Chapter 12- Bills, bills and more bills.

Williams left the hospital having met death in the face, yet again, and came out smiling. I had picked him up and listened to him all the way back to his. I think he expected a brass band and a bunch of helium balloons waiting for him as he stepped outside. If I could have afforded it I would have got them; that's how pleased I was that he had been discharged having been given a clean bill of health. I wish the same could be said for his kitchen. His smile didn't last long however as he put the key in his front door and he struggled to open it. It was being obstructed by a mountain of envelopes. Beige, white, small envelopes, big envelopes were mingled in with papers, flyers and plastic bags from charities asking for donations.

We had to step over the pile just to get into the front room. He stood there unaffected by the pile of what I assumed was bills and asked: "Do you want a brew, mate? I've got more things to worry about that all that". "Would love one, mate", I answered.

"Well you know where the kettle is, mate. Two sugars", he said.

There was never a "please" with Williams. Only once did he ever say please to me; and the circumstances in which that happened are not for your eyes. I told him that, understandably, the bread had gone mouldy and the milk had gone off.

"Good job I've got some Coffee Mate in then. Stop moaning, mate, and just get the bloody brew done!" he shouted from the comfort of his settee.

So I brewed up whilst he put the fire on the lowest setting. The coma hadn't affected him that much; he was still a tight git. I had thought that maybe he would wake up a different person.

Not too much; maybe just a little bit more refined. But no, it was not to be. But to be honest it wasn't too much of a disappointment. He sat down with his brew, put on his glasses (the ones that he thought made him look clever) and started to open the first of the envelopes. The first was a bill from the local authority for the last year's Council Tax.

This was not a good start, I thought.

He opened the next one which was another bill for Council Tax (the year before the one he already owed). And you'll never believe it ....he opened another and there was another demand for the year before that!

They were in the deepest reddest print I had ever seen. The sort of red that means "you're in deep shit." In total he owed three years amounting to over three thousand pounds. Three thousand pound! I asked him why on earth he hadn't paid.

He answered me by saying: "Nobody pays it. I used what I would pay them on Gucci jeans and Stone Island jumpers. Clothes maketh the man, mate. As long as I pay the rent I've got a roof over my head. I thought that's what everybody did. Only yuppies and old married couples pay the council tax in Salford, mate. I'm telling you."

I didn't know what to say. I was stunned into silence. He worked through the pile of envelopes which were mixed with leaflets for window blinds, pizza delivery menus and Stannah stair lifts. He appeared upset when he looked at the one for stair lifts; I guessed it must have reminded him of the escalators that had taken him up to heaven and maybe it had just been too much.

Williams looked as though he had things on his mind. What they were I didn't know. When he had sorted through, the pile of bills was twice as big as the leaflets. He had pulled out the free newspapers and started to look at the four most recent editions of the Salford City Reporter. The first one had the headlines that Salford Reds Rugby Club had been taken over by a multi-millionaire businessman who had promised that he 'would take the club to Wembley within two years.'

Williams did not appear convinced of this claim and said: "He must mean on a day out to watch the Challenge Cup Final 'cos I can't see them ever playing there. Be a good piss up that for 'em. I bet he's taking a fiver a week off them to pay for it." Then he started going on about how the only chance the new owner had of taking a team to play at Wembley was if he was going to buy another club. He convinced himself that the millionaire looked more like a club bouncer from St Helens than the affluent new owner of his home town's rugby club.

I let him go on ....and on.....and on. I would have normally have left his company at that point. I had learnt over the months of our friendship had grown that sometimes Williams was best left alone. He used to tell me when he was tired and that was my cue to go and sometimes I knew it was time for me to leave of my own accord to safeguard my own sanity. But he'd only just left hospital and to be honest I had missed the banter and the sense of being comfortable in each other's company. I also thought it was possible that he might have a relapse. Well let me tell you readers that he very nearly did when he started to read the next edition of the Reporter which had gone to press the week after his accident.

There, on the front page was a picture of his crushed car wrapped around the lamp post. Underneath that picture was a rather unflattering shot of Williams. Somehow the picture had made him look like one of the cast members from One Flew Over the Cuckoo's Nest and he was not happy. Not happy at all.

He said indignantly: "Fuck me! I've told 'em about using that one. It's not my best side that, mate. I've told 'em I'll send 'em a good one in if they want. I'm sure they do it to piss me off. I was gonna frame that as well. Keep it as a memento for the grandkids. "Man crashes car.....miracle escape by Lazarus Williams."

Time to go, Shazza, I decided.

Standing up to leave him to his own thoughts I heard him say: "Eh, what's this one?" He opened the white A5 envelope and smiled before saying: "Oh, it's Darvis Berkins, they've agreed to settle out of court. I best phone my solicitor quick". I heard him on the phone speaking to his solicitor whom I couldn't help but feel sorry for. He must be the most overworked legal representative in the country. And that was just with Williams' cases.

His voice got louder and I heard him say: "What do you mean? What? They're prepared to make an offer that they'll drop it if I drop it? And we'll cover our own costs. Cheeky bastards! I'll see you in court. And don't worry I'll be early". He then proceeded to tell me what his solicitor had said and finally at the end of another long, one-way conversation he told me that there was no way he was going to drop the claim and he assured me that when it got to court it would "sort" the council tax out. He somehow seemed to be back to his old self..........

Do you ever think you know a person inside out? That you know what they're thinking about even if you're not in their company at the time. I knew that at about ten o'clock in the morning that Williams would be thinking about having a brew and the butties he had made the night before. I knew how he folded the aluminium foil over his butties and how he patted the top of them down before he put them in his butty box. I knew that about three hours after having ate his butties he would be thinking about what he could have for his dinner and who he could wind up next. I knew that after that he would probably start thinking about when to pack up and set off back to the yard. I knew when he was worried about something. He worried about things that mattered; important things. So, as the court case loomed I knew he was bothered about something. But he wasn't the sort to worry about trivial things like an impending court case.

I asked what was bothering him as he was uncharacteristically quiet. Well, not quiet; he was never quiet. He was quieter than normal; which meant he still talked non-stop but there was something missing.

It's our Amanda", he said. "She's getting married and it's my job to pay for it all, isn't it?" he added.

I had seen him faced with difficulties before and he had just shrugged them off. Big difficulties. If being charged with thirty plants and ripping off Eon wasn't serious I don't know what is. But this time he looked a little defeated. And I knew why. It was because he didn't want to let her down. His kids meant everything to him and I just knew he would want to give her the wedding she had always dreamed of. But for the first time ever he was, for want of a better phrase, on his arse. I watched him check his lottery numbers and when he didn't win his face was like a little boy's who had watched his favourite Action man get crushed by a ten ton juggernaut.

The day of the court case arrived and he asked me would I wait at the court until the case had finished and then I could drive him home. It wasn't because he wanted support; it was purely to save him bus fare after it had finished. So I watched him enter the front doors of the Civil Courts with his solicitor and sat in the courtroom and waited patiently. Eventually it was Williams' turn to be questioned. He stood there describing the events of what had happened. And for once I knew he was telling the truth.

Darvis Jerkin's solicitor kept firing questions at Williams trying to catch him out but my mate had been in this situation before; and more than once, I can tell you. But their solicitor seemed to be getting angrier and angrier the more Williams wouldn't budge and stuck to his version of events. After this, the judge retired to think about his verdict and I sat with the rest of the viewing gallery to wait.

Williams came back into the room with his solicitor and the judge. He sat down and listened to the outcome. To his horror, the judge had ruled in Jarvis Derkins favour and he could not believe what had happened. Another ruling for the big man fighting the little man. He left the court dejected and didn't say a word. He looked up towards the sky and suddenly it was though he had seen the light.

He smiled and said: "Shazza, I've had an idea. Look at them up there. Tonners, seventeen quid a slate and there must be at least nine thousand of them up on that roof." He then proceeded to walk straight into the Magistrates Court across the road, entered the door and walked up to the reception desk and said to the receptionist: "Look, love, I've been waiting here since nine o'clock for my case. What's happening, love? I've not even been shouted for yet."

"Oh, I think we have called for you Mr. Williams. We've been looking for you all morning. I think there's even a warrant out for your arrest if I'm not wrong," the stern looking woman on the desk replied.

"Well, I've been here in the canteen waiting. I've had twelve brews and three pisses, love, what's been going on?", he said.

Even though I was now accustomed to his bullshitting (or artistic licence as he liked to call it) I still actually believed him sometimes, even though I knew he was lying. Williams' solicitor then appeared, as if by magic.

Williams said to him: "What's going on, Mike? I've been here all morning waiting". "Don't worry", he said. "I know the magistrate and I'll see if I can get you weighed off now. What are we going for? Guilty on both charges?", he asked. "Yes", Williams replied. "And see if you can hurry 'em up, I've been waiting all day"

Even though I knew he had been in the Civil court he walked into the Magistrate's court and his case was dealt with. After an hour, Williams came out with a guilty verdict. He had received a six month tagging order (or a free Ben 10 watch as he was later to tell his children) and a two thousand pound fine for fiddling Eon. But at least he was free.

Chapter 14-An unexpected bonus

My mate returned to work the following day and the first thing he did was to tell the lads his news from the Civil court.

He said to them: "Two fuckin' years I've waited for that to go to court and the bastards lied through their back teeth. Where's the justice in this system, eh?" He then told him the news from the Magistrate's court: "Two grand fine for fiddling the leccy and a Ben 10 watch for six months. Can't go out of the house now after nine. It'll be like being 13 again. Still it'll keep me out of the pub for a bit. I'll save a fuckin' fortune for the kids to spend at Christmas."

He told them all about the previous day's events and then he said " When I came out of the Civil court, you'll never believe what I seen. Nine thousand tonners on that roof, lads. It'd only take us a few hours to get them off. Seventeen quid each! They'd pull me right out of the shit".

Williams' mates, Binnsy and Azza trusted him to the hilt; the same as he did with them. Binnsy said: "It'd pay my mortgage off that, mate."

Azza added: "A few mates are going to Mexico next week. I never booked it cos I was skint. Would have loved to have gone."

Well readers, all I'll say is that four days later, Azza was at First Choice booking an all inclusive, Binnsy had an appointment at the Halifax to pay off his mortgage, and Williams was sending a cheque to his daughter for her big day.

Chapter 15-Wedded Bliss

A month later the wedding was imminent and Williams was getting excited at the thought of giving his daughter away. He was looking forward to being the father of the bride and making his speech. It was a new chapter in Williams' life. He was seeing his children grow and now his eldest was going to make him proud. The recent "unofficial contract" with the Magistrate's Court had enabled Williams to pay for whatever his daughter wanted and he felt a sense of relief knowing he had paid his way.

Well, Williams asked me to go to the wedding as his guest. He said he would take me as a treat for waiting at his bedside during his coma. I was quite pleased as it was in Nottingham and it sounded as though it would be a nice day.

Now Williams would never say anything offensive intentionally but after he had asked me to go as his guest he very bluntly said: "Now listen, mate. I best take you to Selfridges and get you a decent frock 'cos, and I ain't being funny here mate, but I'm sick to death of seeing that skirt and top from Primarni. This is gonna be a posh doo so I'd best smarten you up a bit."

I knew he meant it in a nice way. And after making sure he was paying for a 'decent frock' I can assure you I'm was not gonna refuse a freebie. After three hours of wandering round Selfridges (ten minutes choosing my outfit and two hours fifty minutes choosing his) we came out laden with bags. I only had to mention that my only decent pair of shoes needed re-heeling and he bought me a new pair, I was worried that the effects of the coma had eventually caught up with him. He was the same man; he looked the same and talked the same but some of the worry lines had disappeared from his face. The unexpected bonus had taken years off him.

So the night before the wedding we set off on the two hour drive. Spring had arrived and the drive was relaxing. The motorway was clear and Williams' newly acquired Ford Focus covered the distance smoothly and quickly. The sun was shining as we came off the motorway and travelled along the A roads to his daughter's house. He had been going over his speech on the way down there and was word perfect without the help of a written script. Part of me wanted him to do it off the cuff having had a few Bacardi and Cokes but then another part of me recognised that the "changed" Williams would not want to embarrass his daughter (well not too much anyway).

We arrived at his daughter's house and were greeted by her and her husband to be. There were other people there from both sides of the family and I watched as Williams asked people how they were doing. Later that evening he went out for "a few" with his prospective son-in-law and as he left I could just imagine him going through his speech for the twenty eighth time.

He had known Gary for years and was confident that his daughter was going to be happy. People spoke highly of Williams and even though I tried to gauge just how much everyone had drunk, I was pleasantly surprised that every compliment paid to my mate was genuine.

The next morning came and the sun was out in full force. I went to the church and waited for Amanda to arrive with her dad; my mate Williams. The church was in a quaint village not far from where the bride to be lived. It was a small stone church surrounded by gravestones that looked as though they had been there longer than the village itself. The setting was perfect. The church, the bent headstones, the newly cut grass and the cherry blossom trees lining the path up to the church.

The bride's car pulled up on the road just near the entrance to the church yard. Williams got out of the car and walked round to open the door for his daughter. Amanda stepped out giving everyone their first glimpse of the dress. Williams had commented on the drive down to Nottingham that it had better be a decent wedding frock because it had cost him enough but as Amanda walked down the path I knew he wouldn't feel disappointed. Everybody filed into the church and took their seats. The service was lovely and when the exchange of vows were made I seen Williams filling up as Amanda and Gary looked lovingly into each other's eyes. Williams smiled as the vicar told the beaming bridegroom that he could "now kiss the bride".

The reception was in the church hall adjoining the church. There were beautiful spring flowers placed on every table and as Amanda walked into the hall everyone smiled. I know I've already told you it was perfect but it really was. The meal was lovely and as I surveyed the room I noticed just how happy everyone was. The time came for the speeches.

For once, every word that came out of Williams' mouth was sincere and heartfelt. He made special mention to Azza and Binnsy, who had just arrived as the meal started. and said that without their help the wedding wouldn't have been possible. The trio laughed as they shared their own personal joke.

His speech was a huge success and made people cry and laugh at the same time. He had that effect on people, I knew better than most. The evening reception was just as perfect as the whole day had been. The disco was an eclectic of music varying from the 60s onwards to the Madchester sounds Williams was so familiar with.

Williams approached me from the bar. I could sense that something was about to happen. As he got closer and closer the smile on his face grew bigger and bigger. Suddenly, right in front of me, Williams went down on one knee. My heart was pumping with excitement. Girls, I had waited for this moment since I had first set eyes on that gay photographer. It was as if all my dreams were coming true. Suddenly, Williams was gazing into my eyes. I couldn't believe what was happening. Girls, I was melting right there on the spot.

Then he said: " You know what Shazza? You're never going to believe this. I've torn my fuckin' cartilage."

Hidden Depths:Payback Time

Chapter 20 – Undercover

Two weeks passed and I hadn't heard from Williams since the day of the last visit. There were no letters or phone calls to let me know how he was getting on in the kitchens or how his newly formed football team was doing. I had missed him in the same way I missed Jack Duckworth after Bill Tarmey left Coronation Street. Things carried on without him but something was missing. I couldn't say what it was but there was something not quite right.

Every time my phone rang I wanted it to be Williams but it wasn't. More often than not it was Jonathan. He had started to ring four maybe five times a day just to ask what I was doing or tell me about his day. To be honest I didn't mind. He was interesting to listen to and I suppose charming is the right word to use.

Over the course of two weeks he had grown on me slowly. He had taken me to the pictures and had no qualms about getting me a drink; unlike Williams who wouldn't have bought me a drink if I had just walked across the Sahara for two months and was dying of thirst. He always picked me up in his brand new Audi TT; was always exactly on time and usually brought me a small bunch of flowers on every date.

I couldn't fault him at all. He was the ideal man really. Five feet ten, dark thick wavy black hair, a roman nose and perfect teeth. He wore designer suits that were impeccably cut and fitted perfectly to his well-toned thighs. He made Jose Mourinho look like an overweight tramp. But, in fact he was a bit too perfect.

He had very liberal views on everything and was polite and easy going in everyone's company. He was so politically correct he could have been a Blue Peter presenter whereas Williams would have gone straight in with two feet and I would have been stunned into silence with some of his antics.

Williams made Brian Clough look positively sensitive whereas Jonathan would have never have said anything to offend me. But I wanted to be offended; I wanted to laugh; and more than anything I wanted the sarcasm back that I had with Williams.

I never really got excited about seeing Jonathan, not the way I did when I knew I was going to be in the company of Williams, but I always recognised the fact that other women would have bitten my hand off to have the chance of going out with him. He didn't kiss the way I wanted him to, it was all very polite. He never wanted to get a chip barmcake and just sit on the settee and have a laugh. He always wanted to go to the country for a drive and get a sit down meal. I hated fresh air, the smell of cow dung and sitting down in the middle of loads of other people watching me eat.

Most women would rate him as a nine out of ten, possibly a ten, and sometimes I thought he was perfect; other times he was too perfect.

One day when Jonathan was taking me out for a drive he asked: "Have you heard from the jailbird recently? Has hegot long left to do?"

"Not long now, couple of months", I replied trying to avoid his first question.

"What was it he did again? Something to do with stripping the roof off the Magistrates Court wasn't it? I seen it on the front of the Manchester Evening News," Jonathan said before adding that one of his friends knew the judge who had given Williams his sentence.

When he said those words I felt myself seething. It was as though he took pleasure in the fact that my mate had been caught. "Yes, I believe the MEN sold about an extra ten thousand copies that day because of the Bill and Ben headline", I answered him trying not to laugh. I instinctively knew that Jonathan would not see the funny side of it. When he did laugh his eyes didn't twinkle. It wasn't the same. Half of me wanted to punch his face in as I said it.

That night he dropped me off and, as usual, he got out and went to open my passenger side door and held my hand as I got out. He thanked me for a lovely evening and kissed me. He didn't run his fingers through my hair and make me go weak at the knees and there were no butterflies in my stomach but he was an okay kind of guy.

Sometimes I got the impression he avoided saying my name because it would have offended his middle class sensitivities. I just wanted to hear Williams' voice call me Shazza, but as I said goodnight to Jonathan I came to the conclusion Williams had forgotten me, his loyal mate, and maybe it was time to give Jonathan a chance. He may be boring but he was reliable and he showed he cared.

The next morning the postman delivered a letter. I knew it was Williams' writing and opened it hoping to read that he was doing okay. It was a long one; he must have been bored.

Dear Shazza,

Mate, I've been so busy I don't know whether I'm on my arse or me head. Been shafted over by the guv but I'll tell you about that in a minute. I've got so much to tell you so you better sit down with a brew and three Kit Kats you greedy git!

First of all, let me tell you about my new venture. It's Williams' home brew. It's just like Holt's Regal. It tastes just the same, makes you feel just as rough, it gives you the trots just the same but cost about a tenth of the price! I do it with the yeast that lad from the bakery gives me. In fact we've got quite a little drinking club now. It's just like being in the Wagon and Horses; only the clientele is a bit more refined in here, mate!

A few of the lads off the footie team have tried it but I've told them to lay off it before matches cos I don't want it affecting their performance. The team's doing really well, mate. In fact the governor's really pleased with us. Too fuckin' pleased though, that's the problem. I went up to his office yesterday about my parole. I've kept my head down, Shazza, and I just want to get out now. But I went up and when I asked him if I was set for it he just said he didn't think it was going to be possible. I thought I would be looking at not long to go now but I know why he won't give it me, Shazza. The team's making him look brilliant and he wants me to stick it through till after that semi I was telling you about. Then if we get to the final that's another three week.

He has got me by the balls just so he can keep me as manager. I tell you how bad it is, Shazza. His secretary sat there through it and even she knew I was being done over. It was as though she was taking it all in but she was fuming as well. She's alright. Her name rings a bell. I'm sure she knows someone I know.

I was fuming afterwards. It's funny cos the only thing that calmed me down was when I asked her: "What's your name?" and she said: "Sarah Lane." So I asked her where she lived and she must be from Salford Shazza cos she said: "Down the grid," then I said to her: "What number?" and she said: "Cucumber." Shazza, it was like being a little kid again! Anyway she said leave it with her and she'd try and sort something out. I'm not sure what she means but I think she's on my side.

So the semi is next week and the lads are buzzing now. We're playing some team out Cheshire way. They're supposed to be really good, tough bastards as well. It's all everyone is talking about and Dave and Spaghetti Man are really on form. Dave's probably playing better in here than he was outside. And he's getting paid nothing! Just shows you Shazza, it's more about motivation than it is money. I've got all the team on extra pasta and carbs. That's been okayed by the governor. But to be honest Shazza, I was just hoping to get parole early.

I hope you're alright and Trotty and Nick are looking out for you. How's that knob you're seeing? He's not just a knob; he's a prize knob! Anyway I best go because the home brew is fermenting nicely. In fact if I don't get offered Fergie's job when he goes I might start a little brewing business up when I get out. Enclosed a VO for two weeks Saturday. Don't be late. I ain't got time to be sat around waiting.

Bye.

And with that I re-read the letter and wondered if there was going to be a battle of wills between Williams and the governor.

The Saturday of the visit arrived and as I got ready to be picked up by Azza, I felt as though my friendship with Williams was beginning to ebb away. It was impossible to sustain the warmth of a great friendship through letters and the odd phone call.

His life was different to mine and although I wanted to support him, the very fact that he was inside made it different. I assure you that it would be different if it was you and your best mate. We couldn't bounce off one another's humour when conversation was limited to an hour a month and the atmosphere of a prison visitor's room did not encourage humorous exchanges. Conversations were kept to enquiries about how they were, were they doing enough to keep occupied and was there anything they needed.

At this point I wondered if it was a good idea to make this the last visit and just let go.

Azza beeped his horn (metaphorically speaking of course) and I went out to the car. He asked me how I was getting on with Jonathan and I told him truthfully that it was more of something to do to have a cheap social life than a relationship.

He asked me what Jonathan did for a living and it was at that moment that I realised I wasn't actually sure what he did. I just assumed he was some sort of civil servant but never really wanted to know. It's funny how it didn't matter or maybe I just wasn't interested. I never really wanted to know what he did in the day as I thought I would probably find the details dull anyway.

Why Azza was so interested I didn't know. Azza and Trotty had both seemed to have taken an unnatural interest in

Pope.

We picked Binnsy up on the way and made our way to the prison. We went through the same routine as before but I didn't feel as degraded this time as I realised it was just a process that had to be gone through and it had to be done if you wanted to see someone.

That didn't stop me wanting to punch the living daylights out of the female warden who seemed to take pleasure from the fact she was obviously making me uncomfortable.

We could see Williams sat at the same chair as last time. He looked different this time. Older. I remember after the crash when I had gone to visit him that I had noticed his wrinkles had disappeared from around his eyes, but now they had returned and were etched not just around his eyes but all over his face.

We sat down and Azza asked him: "You alright, mate?"

Williams asked me to go and get four brews from the vending machine for us all. He hadn't changed he still seen certain jobs as women's jobs. Chauvinistic bastard. He would never change.

While I was getting the brews Azza turned to Williams and said: "You'll never guess what, mate. That knob Shazza's seeing is undercover from GMP!"

"Do you know what? I thought he sounded too good to be true", Williams said. Then he added: "I never liked the bastard at school. Just don't say anything to her as I don't want her getting hurt. I'll sort something out so that bastard ends up on a rusty old pedal bike doing his round!"

As I arrived back at the table Binnsy asked Williams: "What's the MIF on your top, mate?"

"Oh, that's Gay Chelsea. Every time I take my bib off he sews something else on it. I'm sure he fancies me. Somehow he heard I was a gay photographer," Williams told us.

"I've heard of MILF but what's MIF?" I asked him.

"I think he's acknowledged the fact that I'm now the

manager in a final and added that bit on", Williams laughed.

BInnsy suggested Gay Chelsea was expressing his feelings and said: " Manager I'd fuck, more like, mate."

Williams was outraged as he suddenly realised why half the prison had been laughing and proceeded to unpick the stitching. "Bastard! I'll have him later!" Williams shouted.

"Yea, we bet you will!" Azza added.

"Shut it, lads. You're not in the fuckin' van at work now you know", Williams said. Williams then told us about a phone conversation he had had that week with his cousin Nick. It turned out that Sarah, the governor's secretary had worked with Nick at Salford Council, years ago, and Williams' intuition was right. She had been fuming that his parole had been denied because of the impending football final and she had provided Nick with some interesting information on the governor.

It turned out that last year a few of her dresses had gone missing from her locker. At the time she thought one of the cleaners had nicked them to put on Ebay and make a few quid but her suspicions were raised when she found some rather gaudy coloured lipstick and American Tan 10 denier tights in the governor's top drawer in his office.

At first she thought her boss may have been seeing a prisoner's wife but when she found a pair of rather smelly size ten patent court shoes under his desk she began to put two and two together.

She put the feelers out and found to her surprise that the respected governor was in fact a transvestite who often frequented the more notorious clubs in the Northern Quarter and the really good news was that his wife didn't know about his tendencies to order from Ann Summers and BHS. Sarah had told all this to Nick last week and Williams thought it was his birthday when Nick had passed the information on to him.

Williams thought then that surely he would be out in four weeks. At the most! Williams then told us he didn't want anyone mithering him next week as it was the final and he had a lot of preparation. There was the team to pick, extra training and he had to decide on his tactics. He told us that after reading Fergie's "My Life," and he knew that that's what all the top managers did. I didn't need to read the book; Williams had more or less told us it word for wordover the last few weeks.

The visit had gone so quickly. Azza, Binnsy and myself hadn't had time to get a word in edgeways (again). Absolutely nothing had changed.

Just as we were about to leave Williams said to me: " Tell your new fella, Pope, that there's fifty grand buried in my mam's garden for when I get out, so he won't be the only one driving round in a Audi TT.The dickhead."

The three of us were puzzled as to why he would tell us that. What was the need to say that? I now began to wonder if he had told me the truth about his stash of money that night when I first met his son.

The months after he had told me about his buried treasure I had been tempted to go and find out if there was anything actually there but I always reflected on the fact that Williams had been there for me. He wouldn't have done the same to me. I was positive of that fact.

We all left the visitor's room a little bit perplexed at Williams' words but never the less I would do as he said. Even if it was just to see the look on Jonathan's face.

Chapter 22 - The Tables are Turned.

The day after the visit Jonathan rang and asked me if I wanted to go to lunch. I hated it when he said lunch. Was what lunch? I hadn't, and still haven't any idea of what lunch is. It was breakfast, dinner, tea and supper where I came from. He had gone to the same school as me and Williams so where the bloody hell lunch came from I didn't know. I could just hear Williams' voice saying " What the fuck is lunch?", and I smiled to myself.

An hour later we were sat eating some pretentious meal in a pretentious restaurant when Jonathan asked me: "How was the jailbird yesterday? Probably got himself another six months added on by now. I never liked him at school. The smarmy bastard".

I nearly told him that Williams had same exactly the same thing about him but decided it would only add to the already strained atmosphere.

I had got to the point where I couldn't tolerate any more and I wanted to know why there was so much animosity between them "What is your beef with him, Jonathan?", I asked him.

"I'll tell you what happened, shall I?" he answered me. "When I was thirteen, me and Williams both entered a competition to describe a new Superhero for DC Comics. Mine was brilliant; absolutely brilliant. The prize was to get a character named after you and you got the outfit especially made. Mine had a Lurex suit and Spandex pants and I spent a week designing it. Williams' entry was called Wonderman and if I say so myself it was nowhere near as good as mine. But Williams' entry won. I was cheated. I was robbed. And I'll never forgive him. I wanted that outfit so much it hurt. I still haven't got over it and his smug grin. Every time he walked past me in Tech Drawing at school he smiled. I could kill him. I had ten sessions of counselling at fifty quid a time and I still haven't got over it. Well, I tell you what, when he comes out of there he'll have nothing. I'll make sure of that," he finished with a voice that was full of anger.

At that point I wanted to tell him that my mate would have plenty to come out to and said: "Actually, you're wrong. He's got a nice little nest egg to come out to. I know for a fact that there's fifty grand buried in his mam's back garden." I then told him I'd seen it myself. I hadn't really but he had annoyed me so much that I wanted to rub it in so told him I knew exactly where it was.

"So where is it then?" he asked.

He seemed to be trying to act vaguely interested but I knew he was more than interested. "t's buried near the little cunt with the fishing rod and the blue hat. If you step down three paces away from the bird bath, it's there," I informed him.

At this point Jonathan appeared to be hanging on to my every word. "That's interesting, Sharon. I wish you wouldn't swear though. It's so unbecoming for a woman", he said.

"I'm just using the exact words he said to me," I answered him.

"Yes, I'm sure you are", he replied.

I couldn't eat anymore. The atmosphere tasted nasty. We left, got into his car and not another word was passed between us.

Within days, diggers and a major incident scene had appeared in Williams' mam's street. Well I say a major incident scene; it was actually one of those marquees things from B & Q that they use on 60 Minute makeover, but you get the picture.

When I heard what had happened I had tried to ring Jonathan but strangely his phone was suddenly unobtainable. The bastard. He had just used me to get to Williams.

As you can imagine Mrs Williams' neighbours' curtains were twitching and everyone wanted to know what was going on.

Rumours of murder, bodies under the patio, bank jobs and fraud were all coming to the surface. Unlike Williams' buried treasure. The digging started straight away and skip after skip were filled with soil from Williams' mam's rear garden. Salford Skip Hire made more money that week than they had done all month. The amount of skips GMP ordered those three days must have entitled them to at least a 30% discount.

DCI Pope (as I later found out he was titled) had given exact instructions of how he had wanted the garden excavating. He had wanted them to dig in stages, stepping down from the gnomes to the bird bath.

The digging carried on for days with Williams' mam appearing every now and again carrying her best china teapot saying:" Tea anyone? There's some bourbons there if you like them. Sugar's in the bowl. I've got some custard creams and some jammy dodgers if you want them. I'll bring them out. I was saving them for our Simon but I think I'll get him something a little more special than that for when he comes out. I might get him some him garibaldi's...or do you know what...I'll get him some of the posh ones from Sainsbury's. The ones he likes with the silver foil. Bless his little cotton socks....Mind you, he's not so little now, size eleven feet he's got Jonathan. What are you if you don't mind me asking? About a seven I would imagine", Mrs Williams said with a twinkle in her eye, relishing every moment of having the GMP's finest in her home.

"Do you know I might even make you some butties. I've got a tin of Spam there I've never used and some beetroot that needs using up. You can have that because you need to keep your strength up for all this digging", she added.

While Mrs Williams had been talking, Pope had been staring intently at a gold gilt framed Lowry on the old lady's living room chimney breast wall. He wondered if it was the original that had been stolen from Salford City Art Gallery years before. He was intrigued to know the truth.

"Can I ask you where you got the picture from please, Mrs Williams?", Pope asked Williams' mam.

"Oh, that. It was from Salford flea market. Wednesdays, Fridays and Saturdays", she informed Pope.

" Are you sure, Mrs Williams?", Pope asked.

"Oh, I'm absolutely positive, DCI Pope. It's not an original if that's what you're asking. Look, you can see a bloke there on the way to the factory holding a Nokia N9!" Mrs Williams smirked.

"I wouldn't put anything past your son, Mrs Williams", Pope replied.

After three days of digging and countless skips being filled Williams' mam's garden suddenly had the foundations for a beautifully stepped patio area.

It was just what she had always wanted. Yet, strangely there was no sight of any money. No black bin bags, no holdalls or weather resistant tin boxes. Pope was furious at the fact that not only had he wasted so much time at Mrs Williams' house but he had also been made to feel inadequate as a man by a 70 year old woman.

Pope was summoned to see his bosses straightaway. He would be lucky if he still had a job in the force. He had wasted taxpayers money and police time. Salford Skips were overjoyed, however his bosses weren't. Pope was instantly suspended from all duties and his Italian suit wearing, Audi driving days were over. He was demoted to patrolling the notorious Brookhouse estate on a rusty old bike. He was the laughing stock of the force and also Gameways prison.

I never seen him again. And more to the point I never wanted to. Williams didn't know at this stage what had gone on but I'm sure he had a sneaky idea.

A couple of days later I received a letter from Williams. Again it was lengthy, so I made a brew, sat down, got myself comfortable and started to read its contents.

Hiya Shazza,

How's things? How's it going with your new fella? Haha. I always knew you were too good for that dirty rat. The worm. I hope my mam's pleased with the foundations and the GMP haven't let me down. I heard it took them three days to shift all that soil.

I heard Pope has been suspended. Binnsy told me what had gone on. Serves Pope right. Trying to lead you up the garden path like that. So I thought I'd lead him up the garden path. The knob. Knew he'd fall for that old classic. Saved me mam thousands of pounds as well. Will you ask Binnsy to order the flags as soon as you can from Darvis Berkins? Might as well get the job finished for summer and then she can sit out and enjoy the fruits of GMP's labours.

Well only three weeks now and I'll be out. I won't say I'm counting the hours because I've got the Cup Final coming up on Saturday.

I've been given the nod to see the governor on Friday so I might be out sooner. I expect that's what he wants to see me about. Anyway I've got some big news for you. You'll never believe who's been brought in. Timothy Worrall Armstrong Thompson, or twat for short as we're calling him. He was on the hospital wing when I went to get some bandages for the match.

Anyway we got talking and he told me he'd been given eighteen months for fiddling the tax on his vet business and then he proceeded to tell me a bit of his story. He told me that he'd only married his new wife Rose for tax reasons.

He said that some time before they got married, she was going to meet a lad she knew from school but when the lad didn't turn up to meet her Worrall seized the chance and asked her to marry him. And she said yes. He then told me the story got even better. He told me the poor chap had ended up crashing his car into a lamp post and it was a miracle that he survived. "Poor sod", he had said.

But then he said that the poor guy's misfortune was his gain. I had asked him what had happened to the lad and he started going on that the lad had been caught nicking slates off the Magistrates' Court and how it had made the front page of the MEN and how when he and his wife had read it, they had laughed at the lengths some people would go to in order to make money.

He told me that his friend, a magistrate who was based at the courts, was fuming and then he explained how they had spoke about it over a meal one evening. Then he went on to tell me that although he had friends in a high places it wasn't enough to get him off a charge of tax fraud of nearly two hundred grand. So, Shazza, we are both in here for roughly the same thing. Costing the taxpayer thousands. Only mine involved a lot more graft than his.

Anyway Shazza, I have enclosed a VO. Come on your own next Saturday.

Chapter 24 - Nearly There

The following week seemed to fly by and the next visit came around quickly. I arrived alone, as requested by Williams, and as soon as I walked into the reception area I noticed Rose stood there looking anxious and uncomfortable with the strange surroundings.

I went up to her and asked was she okay. I don't know whether she remembered me from school or just thought I was a friendly face in a room full of strangers.

She told me she was nervous so I tried to reassure her that I was too on my first visit. I didn't ask any questions as to who she was visiting because I already knew all the details. I felt sorry for her because I knew how she would be feeling.

She told me she visiting her husband.

Part of me felt sad that she was standing by someone who had married her for all the wrong reasons and she was probably still unaware of the fact. She then asked me who I was visiting and I told her that she would probably know him. I told her that I was Williams' friend and knew all about the fact that he had been on his way to meet her that eventful night.

Rose mentioned that she knew Williams was in the same prison as her husband so I suggested that it may be a good idea to try and see him to talk about what had happened. Part of me wanted her to talk to him so they could eventually met and see how they felt about one another, but part of me wondered why she had not waited to see why he had not turned up that night. Why had she not trusted him? Why had she married so quickly? She should have given him the benefit of the doubt.

And when I remembered what Williams had said about

how she had laughed about his antics on the Magistrates' Court's roof I wondered whether it was a genuine laughter at Williams' sheer nerve or a mocking laughter. For my mate's sake I didn't want to know.

I thought it best just to let things take their natural course and for him to find that out for himself.

I said goodbye and reassured her that she would be okay. I then watched her walk towards the waiting prisoner.

Williams was sat waiting for me and his first words were: "You're late. Sit down, quick. I've got loads to tell you. Where do you want me to start? You'll never guess what? We won the final. 3-0. There was a thirty yard volley from Dave. A penalty was saved by Spaghetti Man. Then we got two in the second half. Shazza, the atmosphere made the Nou Camp look like Agecroft Cemetery. It was amazing and it was all down to my tactical know how and Dave's Premiership experience plus a few big long balls up front."

Then he carried on with his tale: "I went for the old pyramid formation at the start and the changed to 4-4-2 at half time as Fergie did in the semis against Juventus,99, page 104 My Life. It worked a treat. Dave got out on Friday. He's promised me 10% of his book sales and true to his word he's got Joel a trial. So, for the first time in Joel's life he's got the only trial he's ever wanted to go to," Williams continued. He didn't even give me chance to ask any questions.

"The governor agreed to let me out next Monday after we won. He was made up cos the prison looks good and he's got a trophy in his office. I didn't even have to mention the fact I knew about his Birdcage antics. It's amazing who you know in life and not what you know. I can't wait to try my new homebrew out when I get out. I'm gonna call it Salford Riddles, Shazza. The riddle is everyone will be trying to suss out what's inside it. It's an old Salford brew", Williams said.

"I've heard that Pope's riding round on a rusty old bike.

Serves him right. The bastard. My mam's made up with her new raised patio. Cost a fraction of the price and half the labour. I believe the lads have done a cracking job on it. And by the way mate, I've got to tell you this; my stash was buried in the front garden not the back. They had been walking over it every day. It's under the driveway. Buried it when I did some flagging for her the other month", he said finally drawing breath.

It didn't last long. He soon started again by asking: "Why are you a bit late, Shazza?"

"I've been talking to Rose in the reception. Her husband is in for fraud. She looked a bit nervous so I told her she'll get used to it", I answered him.

Timothy Worrall Armstrong Thompson then beckoned Williams over and said to him:"I hear you're out next week, Williams. I've got a roof that needs stripping and I've heard that you and your gang is one of the best in the business."

Rose fumbled nervously in her handbag; she was obviously anxious about Thompson finding out the connection between her and Williams. She passed Williams a card with her home number on, trying not to look him in the eye. She knew that he would ring as soon as he had been released.

Thompson asked how soon he could do it and when he would get in touch with Rose, to which Williams replied that he would get in touch a couple of days after he got out.

Suddenly I knew that Williams thought Thompson wasn't such a twat after all.

Williams come back to the table and I asked him what all that was about.

"Oh, he's only gone and given me Rose's number not realising who I am and I don't think she wanted him to know either", he said.

"Well, are you going to phone her?" I asked him.

"Just let me get out first, will you. Before you start moaning", he retorted. "Make sure you're at the gates when I get out at nine o'clock and don't be late. I've got a busy day Monday. I've got to go and see the probation officer", he added. And with that the warden announced the end of visiting and I left.

Chapter 25 - Sweet and Sour

I was waiting at the gates for what seemed to be an eternity when finally, Williams appeared smiling.

"Not bad that, Shazza. It went pretty quick. I'm back and I can't wait to have a pint of Holt's Regal in The Wagon", he said to me enthusiastically. "Do you know what, mate? People pay a fuckin' fortune to go to places not as good as this. You know what I mean? These health farms and spas and boot camps. And all they have to do is get themselves a nice little sentence and they can come out of there as fit as a fiddle and full of knowledge," he said.

Full of bullshit more like, I thought.

As we drove back Williams prompted me to pull over saying: "Just let me get some Sterling Super Kings, mate. I haven't half missed them."

He ran inside, returned to the car and opened the packet as quickly as he could. He sat down, lit the cigarette and said: " Oh, I've missed you baby!"

It was at that moment that I wished he hadn't got his parole. He had only been out five minutes and he was beginning to get on my nerves.

Then he said: "Let's go to Brookhouse and see if we can see Pope on his bike".

Against my better judgement I reluctantly drove him to the notorious estate.

Williams very quickly spotted Pope and couldn't contain his excitement saying: "There he is, Shazza. Drive over there quick!"

I pulled up alongside Pope on his bike and Williams wound

down the passenger side window and yelled: "Promotion eh, Pope?"

"Oh, you're out are you Williams? " Pope asked looking enraged at Williams' comments.

"Yea, mate. Just going to find some buried treasure at my mam's. Oh, by the way, my mam said thanks for all your hard work. They quoted her two grand at Dooper Clarke's so you saved her a fortune and she's made up with the job", Williams said adding insult to injury to Pope's wounded ego.

Pope looked as though he was having a hernia and shouted back: "I'm not going to forget this, you know that!"

"My mam said your gang worked like Wondermen," Williams added laughing. He just couldn't resist one last attack.

"Shazza was wondering why you haven't been answering your phone. Is it because you've been demoted? You knobhead! You fell for the oldest trick in the book", he said to Pope.

We then drove back to Williams' house and when we entered through the front door there was a mountain of bills that had built up over his six month vacation. Williams said: "Let's have a brew. It'll have to be tea though. The coffee's harder than Mad McGuire".

He slowly decided to go through the bills one at a time and when he finally finished adding up his outstanding debts it came to just over three thousand pounds. He then seen a letter from his employers LPD saying he was required to start back at work on Monday. The letter ended with the words " Don't be late, Williams. Nick."

Williams asked me could he lend my mobile so he could make a call. Williams said: "Can I start back tomorrow, Nick? I've been on holiday for six months."

I heard Nick's voice saying to Williams: "Yea. You've never been late, never had a day off sick and always worked hard. I don't think there will be a problem."

Williams' face lit up as he realised he would be back at

work the next day with his mates. God help them I thought. He will be boring them rigid with his stories about how he basically ran the prison single handed.

The next day Williams was greeted back at work by two familiar faces; Bill and Ben. He told them how his time inside had gone really quickly and how they owed him a debt of gratitude and six month's lost wages. That day they were sent on a job getting a lorry load of slates back to the yard and Williams took the opportunity to talk non-stop.

Williams asked them what they had been up to since he had last seen them. Predictably, Azza said: "The gym, chillin and following that smarmy git Pope about in his Audi TT for you!"

Binnsy informed Williams that he had been working like a Trojan to save up and buy two more prams for his new grandkids.

After catching up with his mates' news Williams decided it was time to tell them about his dilemma.

For once he had a problem which he shared with his mates.

He told them about how Timothy Worrall Armstrong Thompson wanted them to strip his roof but he didn't have a clue who he was when he had asked him to do the job. He also knew that getting in touch with Rose would upset Shazza, so he asked the lads for advice and said: " What do you think I should do?".

"If you phone in work's time she isn't going to know", Binnsy said.

"I don't know", said Azza. "What do you think?"

"If I knew the answer to that I wouldn't be asking   you two would I?" said Williams.

A week later Williams arrived at Rose's house after making the decision to phone her. He knocked at the door and Rose answered. The moment he had waited for for years had finally arrived.

Williams went into the house and the first thing Rose said was: "Thank you for not saying anything when he asked you to do the roof".

"Well, I was hardly going to tell him was I? Rose, just tell me why you didn't wait to see why I didn't turn up that night", Williams asked her.

"I know, I made a huge mistake. I thought you hadn't come and I reacted on the spur of the
Minute," Rose replied. "It was only that night that I agreed to get married because I thought you had
stood me up."

"But you should have known me better than that," Williams replied. "I don't know how long you have been seeing him for, but he's not right for you," he added.

"Do you think I don't know that now? I'm sick of having fancy dinner parties for all his so called chums,", she said.

"I thought Chum was dog food?" he answered.

Sometimes, I wish that was what I had served up to them," Rose added.

"So, how much does he expect to pay for this job then? I know he's got a few bob," Williams asked.

"Well, he did have until the taxman started noseying about. So, now he doesn't want to pay more than two grand", Rose said.

"Do you want us to move the slates so you don't have the mess?", Williams asked, his mind shifting to more monetary thoughts. Williams worked out that there was six grand in this job. Two grand each for him and the lads, for two days work. Not bad, he thought. His mind wondered back to how he was working in the prison for £8.57 a week (with overtime). He smiled.

Chapter 26 - No Insurance

Williams and the lads arrived for work at Rose's house bright and early the following Saturday. He wore the cleanest high visibility jacket you'd ever seen and even had the audacity to write "Gaffa " in black marker pen across the back of the jacket. He wasn't even aware of the fact that he had spelt it wrong.

Binnsy and Azza got on the roof as Williams started talking to Rose saying: "It will take us two days, we'll strip the front today and the back tomorrow. Is that okay? And it's two coffees, one tea. Two sugars in each. And don't embarrass yourself by forgetting the ten o'clock brew", he instructed her. Williams then ascended the ladder to join the other two lads on the job.

As they were working Williams asked Binnsy what he was going to spend his cash
on, to which Binnsy replied: "A romantic weekend for two with my missus in London. A top hotel as well, mate."

"What about you, Azza?", Williams asked his other colleague

"Feel another holiday coming on, mate", Azza replied.

"You have more holidays than Judith Chalmers, you mate." Williams commented.

Azza was puzzled; uncertain, because of his youth, of who Judith Chalmers was, while Binnsy laughed.

"What about you, mate?" they both asked.

Williams who replied: "The kids and the grandkids as usual!"

The two days passed and eventually all the roof was stripped. The lads looked at the loaded wagon and smiled at the thought of an easy six grand.

Williams spoke to Rose and assured her that he would come round to speak to her the following day. He leant over and kissed her gently as he said goodbye.

The trio set off and the wagon eventually reached the yard, parked up and the men got out. Williams told his two mates to get off home. He needed time to think and offloading the slates on his own would be the perfect opportunity.

The lads had gone, leaving Williams alone in the yard. Just then, one of Williams' bosses, Joe Egerton drove into the yard and parked up. He walked over to Williams and said:

"Williams, I just wanted you and the lads to know that I officially handed my notice in today. I got an accumulator up at Kempton last week and, well, it was quite a tidy amount, I can tell you. Was nearly as much as my privates."

At this comment Williams' head nearly fell off and he said: "God, it must have been a few quid then!"

Egerton carried on: "So, it's made me decide to buy a little cottage in Cornwall. Got a lot of mates from the Army down there so I can meet up with them and take it easy from now on. Williams, you know sometimes, you have to remind yourself about what's important in life"

Williams felt it was a rather odd moment.

The slateyard could be quite an eerie sort of place at night and this was one of them moments where everything was peaceful but a little bit surreal. He would be sorry to see Egerton go but he felt that he was meant to hear his words of guidance before he left.

And with that Egerton's car pulled away and Williams was left to offload the wagon.

So, after a laborious hour, the slates were stacked like dominoes and Williams finally sat down to contemplate his future while he waited to be paid out for the slates. His mind was torn. He didn't know who he loved the most. He didn't want to hurt Shazza or Rose as he loved them both immensely.

He was thinking one moment he was telling Rose he wanted to be with Shazza and the next minute he was telling Shazza he wanted to be with Rose.

The choice was tearing him in half. Did he go with his first love? Or did he go with his new love?

He slowly pulled out another Super King and thought to himself: "I'll tell ...." Suddenly, the sound of screeching tyres could be heard from around the corner.

Williams was sat on the slates lighting his cigarette. He inhaled slowly, still thinking; his mind had changed yet again.

The car door opened swiftly and out jumped Winston Obanga, the six foot six Inhabitant of Moss Side who Williams had crossed several years ago.

Suddenly, Williams had a flashback to when he had totalled the man's Mercedes People carrier with his seven ton truck.

The man approached Williams and said: "You've got no fuckin' insurance now, man!" He then proceeded to pull out his revolver, pointed it and fired indiscriminately.

Williams caught one in the leg, one in the arm, one in the chest and one in his hand. He then slumped to the floor and lay in a pool of blood.

A red river flowed away from his wounded body.

The car door slammed shut and sped off as fast as it had arrived.

His cigarette was still burning; still held lightly between his fingers.

In the yard, a dark shadow came out of the office. It was the man who had come to give Williams the money for the offloaded slates. He had just been about to approach Williams and hand over the money when he had seen the car drive into the yard and he had heard the commotion.

The shithouse had hid behind a big pile of Yorkshire like a man waiting for a bailiff's knock at the door. He had narrowly escaped being hit by a stray bullet which had ricocheted off one of the slabs.

After the gunman had left the yard the man ran into the office, rang for an ambulance, grabbed some towels, then swiftly ran over to Williams' unmoving body and held the towels as firmly as he could against the wounds to stem the furious flow of blood.

Within minutes, the ambulance had arrived.

Williams' body was lifted into the back of the vehicle and the ambulance left the yard with its sirens wailing.

It sped through the streets at an alarmingly fast rate as the driver was aware that Williams' life hung in the balance.

The ambulance quickly arrived at the A & E department and Williams was rushed inside where a crash team was waiting for his arrival.

Within minutes Williams had been given a blood transfusion and the flow of blood was stemmed. Fortunately for Williams, one bullet had gone right through his shoulder without hitting any nerves; one bullet was lodged in his arm; one went right through his hand and the one that had lodged in his chest was removed successfully.

The surgeon emerged from the operating theatre after three hours and announced that Williams was going to be okay.

Yet again, much to the annoyance of the Salford Royal Hospital nurses. In fact Nurse Hookway was getting so disgruntled at Williams' Lazarus like ability to come back from the dead that she asked for a transfer to another Health Authority.

Her exact words, one of the ward nurses informed me, were "I'd rather be nursing fuckin' Scousers in Walton General than that annoying little bastard!"

Anyway, Williams had pulled through and a week later he

was back in the slate yard collecting the money that was owed him and the lads.

That morning he had rang to tell me he was returning to work and said: "It's a good job he didn't pay me before I got shot because anything could have happened to that money. I wouldn't mind betting it would have gone straight back in his safe, the robbin' bastard"

"This is the man who saved your life, mate", I reminded him.

To which he replied; "He could have thrown some cobbles at Obanga orsomething. He was probably scared of damaging them, the tight bastard."

So, Williams had cheated death yet again. You'd think that a man who had come near to meeting his maker on two occasions might have acquired a sense of humility. No, you'd be wrong. He was just the same, unfortunately. The only difference was, that his finely chiselled body was now beginning to resemble SpongeBob Square Pants.

Chapter 27 - The Decision

Williams now realised for once in his life who and what was important. I don't know whether it was his near death experience or the words of Joe Egerton that had helped him.

For once he started to have a serious conversation with me.

"Shazza, do you know what? The way I'm going I don't think I'm going to see my kids getting married or my grandkids grow up for that matter." He then added: "Shazza, let's go out for a meal. Make sure you bring your purse and don't forget your credit card. I don't want you embarrassing yourself not having enough cash on you to pay. Oh, and you can drive cos I fancy a drink to celebrate my second coming."

That's funny I thought, remembering one particularly disappointing night, I wasn't aware of there actually being a first. But I kept my thoughts to myself; as you would.

As the weeks went by Williams and I grew closer and closer. He never mentioned Rose any more. It was as though he had realised who really did care for him. It had taken him a long time to see what I could see all along.

He had found true love at last. He was no longer just in love with himself. I knew it was only a matter of time before he was going to get down on one knee. I knew that this time I was not going to be humiliated. This time there was not going to be a torn cartilage in sight.

When he did ask me I even had the cheek to make him suffer and I paused before I answered.

Williams couldn't wait to tell the lads at work his good news. The only difficulty came in choosing between Bill and Ben as to who to have as his best man.

Williams decided that Binnsy would be great at being a best man as he had travelled all over Europe on stag doos in that role. But he also felt an affection for young Azza as he had taught him everything he knew since he had joined PLD.

He spent more time thinking about this than he did about choosing between Rose and Shazza. The only thing he talked about at work was who was going to be the best man. Williams said he was open to bribes and found himself inundated with Cadbury's Mini Rolls from Binnsy and Hula Hoops off Azza.

In the end he couldn't decide so he chose both. In making this decision he realised he would get two decent presents rather than just one. Over the next few weeks I took (no, dragged is the word) Williams to wedding events all over the North West. We probably spent more on petrol than some people do on their actual weddings.

We got the best that money could buy. The dress, stationery and suits were all bought. The final thing to be purchased was the bouquets which we got from Laura and Gareth's Flowers, a really upmarket shop in Irlam. The owners couldn't do enough for us. It's surprising isn't it what having a little bit of money does where service is concerned.

Williams had to do a little bit of flagging at his mum's house to recover the stash under the driveway in order to meet the escalating cost of the wedding.

His mam was a little bit anxious and even asked him why

he wanted to redo the front pathway as it had only been done two years before. Williams informed her that he wanted it to match the great work that had been done in the back garden.

So most of the items were purchased for the forthcoming nuptials and all of them were paid for up front, in cash.

I had not realised how expensive things were and the final bill was £20k. Williams told me he was going to hide the remaining cash under his bed and if I needed anything just to help myself.

Williams had changed over the past year. He had gone from putting biro marks on the vodka bottle to make sure I didn't drink any without him knowing, to saying I could have anything I wanted.

Don't get me wrong it was a lovely feeling for someone to say that to you but the very essence of what made him what he was, was disappearing. I wasn't sure who he was anymore. It wasn't exactly like a Clarke Kent/Superman scenario (don't for one minute put that image in your heads),but there was definitely a transformation of some kind.

The weeks passed quickly and the day of the wedding finally arrived. Williams had decided to stick to the tradition of not seeing the bride on the morning of the wedding and decided to stay at Binnsy's house.

He told me that he thought it was bad luck to see the bride just before the ceremony but I knew it was more to do with the fact that Binnsy had purchased three crates of Stella and three litre bottles of Smirnoff and the plan was that it was all to be consumed the night before.

So three hours before the wedding I was alone at his house. I looked around and realised that his house was to become my home.

My mind was in torment. I didn't know what to do. I looked back at how our relationship had developed over the past year.

Williams had always had the upper hand. He said; I did. He said jump; I asked how high. He offended me; he apologised; I accepted his apology straightaway. I offended him; I apologised; he accepted my apology after three weeks.

I looked at the beautiful dress hung up on the wardrobe door. I looked at the bag with thirty grand in it. Lovely crisp purple notes with our sovereign smiling at me. I wondered what she would have done. I looked back at the dress then back at the bag.

This went on for several minutes before I came to a decision. He had always held the trump card. But now the worm had turned and I had the trump card.

In fact I had thirty thousand of them.
The Bentley we ordered the week before pulled up outside and the chauffeur looked puzzled as I got in the back passenger seat. He drove off in the direction of the church and after driving for a couple of minutes he pulled up to stop at red lights. The driver flicked the indicator switch to signal that he was going to turn right. It was another crossroads moment.

Do I turn right into uncertainty and hurt? Into a life that would have its fair shares of highs and most certainly have its fair shares of lows. Or do I turn left and have a life of predictability?

I told the driver to take a left turn instead of right.

Within ten minutes the car was arriving at Terminal Two at Manchester Airport. The flight I had booked the previous day to the Maldives was due to depart in three hours time....

Meanwhile Williams was waiting at the church with all the guests. He kept checking his watch and although each moment was an eternity the minutes were passing and the more time passed the more he started to imagine why I hadn't arrived.

He knew being late was part of the tradition but he knew I was always punctual and never let him down. Perhaps that was part of the problem.

"What's the normal time for a bride to be late, Binnsy?" Williams asked his best man.

"Don't worry, mate. She'll be here in a minute" Binnsy reassured him. "She'll be having a quick Baileys if I know Shazza," he added trying to pacify the bridegroom.

"Ok, I'll have another ciggy then, "Williams said.

Feeling slightly more confident. After he lit his fifth cigarette of the day he said: "I've got a funny feeling, mate".

"You should have mate. It's your wedding night tonight. But in case you're worried I've got some of them blue diamonds if you need 'em, mate," Binnsy offered.

"I don't need them, mate. I'm the human scaffolding pole! I've put many a bird in Salford Royal A & E with stomach cramp!" Williams informed his bestman.

They both laughed. I know what you're thinking readers; he's a bloody idiot. Well, you'd be right. But he's my mate and only I'm allowed to think that. I know him better than most and the part of him that is an idiot is far outweighed by the part of him that isn't.

"I can't see any sign of the car, mate", Williams muttered.

It was then that Binnsy offered to ring my phone.

Williams told him to go ahead.

So, Binnsy rang my phone and I answered. I could not be heard as the airport tannoy announcement drowned out my voice. All Binnsy could hear was: "All passengers for Flight 332 for the Maldives please make their way to gate 6. This is your final call".

When the announcement had finished and Binnsy could hear me, I said: "Binnsy, tell him I'm dead sorry and I do love him, more than he'll ever know, but tell the bastard now he knows how it feels. How I felt at Amanda'swedding!"

And with that I made my way to Gate 6. I had a plane to catch and thirty grand to spend.

Chapter 29 - Buy it Now

I woke up and found myself lying on soft, white, powdery sand, basking on a sun drenched beach in paradise. The sun was warming my face and I could feel the sand between my toes. I felt alive. I had a crisp, cool drink by my side and I finally felt myself beginning to relax under the warm rays of the midday sun. But my relaxation was disturbed when suddenly the seriousness of what I had done hit me.

Why had I done it? Had I not thought of the repercussions? What had made me think I could possibly get away with it? My mind started to wonder back to that day when, for the first time in my life, I finally plucked up some courage. I thought back to the day that should have been my wedding day. It was two weeks ago. I thought back as to how I had left my husband to be stood at the altar with all 300 of our guests waiting in the aisles and how I had taken his life savings from under his bed.

I felt sick when I thought about all those people who had bought outfits and presents, had travelled quite a distance to the wedding and finally they expected a lovely meal and a good piss up. But still, I was happy and I had done the right thing. Well, I was 98% sure that I had done the right thing.

The thirty grand in my suitcase made me even more sure that I had made the right decision. It wasn't just my husband to be that I had left standing there at the church that day; my husband to be was my best mate as well.

My best mate; Williams.

My mind was working overtime. Why did I ask the wedding car driver take that left turn instead of going straight to the church? More to the point, why had I taken 30 grand of my mate's money? I'll tell you why? Because I deserved some happiness and if I found it in some muscular handsome Latino male on a tropical beach then so be it.

Williams had disappeared from out of my mind as quickly as he had entered it in the first place. The only time I had ever thought about him since that day was when I caught sight of a Smirnoff bottle tempting me on the top shelf of the beach hut bar which I had been frequenting for the last two weeks.

It was unforgivable, but I felt it was the least I deserved after putting up with his ways and his actions over the last eighteen months. What is it they call them? Annoying bloody habits. And believe me; they were very annoying. I don't know how I put up with them to be honest.

But sometimes having him as a mate cancelled out all the annoying things. But that day we should have got married, I had been tempted by thirty thousand pounds. I had a bag full of money as my reward for putting up with his stupid jokes and his outrageous behaviour. But part of me was wondering how he had reacted when he found out that I had not only jilted him at the altar but also taken his little stash.

Part of me found it all very amusing but the other part of me felt scared that he wouldn't quite see the funny side of it.

He had taken part in some of the biggest scams going (some of which failed, disastrously, some of which he managed to pull off) so I thought he may have secretly admired the sheer audacity of my work.

I knew sooner or later that one day I would find out exactly what he thought.

The day I had left, Williams had been put in a position that he was made to tell our guests that I wouldn't be turning up at the wedding. I felt sad thinking about how embarrassing it must have been but also found myself laughing when I imagined his bewildered face when he discovered that I had taken his bag of treasure. I could just imagine the words he would have said when he seen the money had gone and take my word for it they would not have been "Oh, dear!".

There had originally been 50 grand in the little bag under his bed but I had quickly made a large dent in that by spending nearly 20 grand on the wedding. I had ordered the best of everything and had spared no expense.

You may be wondering why I had spent all that money when I had no intention of turning up. Well, to be honest I did have every intention of turning up. Do you think I'd be so stupid to waste all that money and by doing so reduce my little holiday fund?

It was a couple of days before the wedding that I began to realise that the whole marriage thing would have been the equivalent of placing a long odds bet on a three legged horse in the National. Anyway, I couldn't change what I had done and I'd like to say I was getting bored with the surroundings of my new home but I would be lying. It was idyllic. I was in the Maldives and it felt like heaven on earth. However, it all changed on the sixteenth day of my stay.

I received a letter with a Manchester postmark in the right hand corner dated a week earlier. I hastily opened it worried about what it contained.

It read: Dear Shazza, Just a very short one to let you know that Williams is bloody livid. He's started to flog all the pressies from the wedding (well, I know the wedding didn't happen but Williams said he's keeping them as they were given in good faith).

He's got them all on Ebay and he's flogging them at a third of what they're worth on Buy it Now options.

I know he's my mate, but if I were you I would make

yourself scarce there because he really wasn't happy. It wasn't the fact you stood him up Shazza; it was the 30 grand he's bothered about. Anyway, I reckon he will be out there in the next week as he's taking up every loan going from Mr Wonga and Pay Day.com. He's been singing " Mr Wonga, I'll get my Wonga back off her. The cheeky bitch!"

Hope you get this letter somehow. I rang a few hotels in the Maldives and finally found you. Hope you're okay and soaking up the sun. Serves him right, the moaning old bastard!

Take care mate, Binnsy.

So, Williams was on his way was he? Bastard. Didn't take him long. In fact, at the very moment I finished reading the letter, he was in Co-Op Travel on Salford Precinct booking a cancellation flight to the Maldives for the following day. He had sold all the presents (and I mean ALL the presents; even the new coasters his Nanna had given us that she had got from Poundland) and he had plenty of money to play with.

He entered the travel agents as soon as the assistant had turned the Closed sign to Open, walked up to the desk and sat down, eager to get the earliest flight possible.

In fact he was that keen he had gone with his suitcase, his passport and was wearing his cut off denim shorts and sunglasses. What a knob!

He said to the assistant: "What have you got going out to the Maldives, love? As soon as possible. Today, if you can".

"Let me have a look and I'll see what I can do. Just give me a couple of minutes", she replied.

Williams couldn't get his words out quick enough and said: "Look, love. Time's money and I can't be waiting around. She's out there with thirty grand of my money and I need to get it back!"

"Who is, Mr Williams?" the girl asked curiously.

"You never mind. Just find me a flight, love."

"Hang on, I can get you one for tomorrow at two o'clock.

Is that okay? ", she asked.

"Yea, yea, yea, just book it. Here's the cash," Williams said to her.

"Oh, I'm sorry Mr Williams, we can't take cash. Allthese forgeries knocking about. We only take cards now," she advised him.

"Right, can I leave my suitcase here. I'm going to have to get to the bank and pay all this in", he said.

"Yes, ok then. If you must," she answered him.

Williams then dashed round to the bank where he stopped abruptly when he seen a big queue. He waited his turn but all the time was trying to push in to get to the front. Just as he was about to be served one of the cashiers shut her till and pulled the shutter down at her counter.

Williams found himself behind an old woman who seemed to have taken all her one and two pence pieces to be counted and paid into her account.

The young man behind the other counter started to weigh the first of the bags she handed over to him. There must have been at least two hundred pounds in her little tartan bag on wheels.

Williams was now purple with rage.

An hour later he was finally served by the young man who said: "Sorry for the wait, sir."

"And they wondered why they get mugged!" Williams shouted.

"She's a customer just like you, sir. We're here to help everybody and anybody," he smiled patiently.

Williams then paid the proceeds of his Ebay sales and Wonga loans into his account.

After finishing the transaction the assistant said to Williams: "Can you step into the manager's office please?"

"I've not got time, honestly," Williams replied.

"It'll only take a minute. The manager just wants to see

you," the young man said, not one to be put off.

Williams then stepped into the office and two minutes later the GMP had arrived asking Williams how he had managed to pay so much money into the bank in one transaction.

He told them that he was going on holiday to get over his recent heartache and he didn't trust using Euros. He said to the police: "You know what it's like, mate. You can't trust them Greeks or Spiks. I've seen them rioting on the telly. I'd rather have my money in the bank. Is there a problem?"

With this, the police left the bank frustrated by Williams ability to leave make them look like fools. Again.

Williams then raced back round to the travel agents and waited in a newly formed queue for the assistant who was dealing with his flight.

"Right, love, let's get this flight booked," Williams said.

"Right, I'll see if it's still there," she said logging back into the screen. "Oh, I'm very sorry, that flight's gone. We can't do anything for another three days," the assistant said, dreading Williams' reaction.

She was right to dread it. He was exasperated and his head was literally about to fall off. The thought of me spending all his money on alcohol, fine dining and other basic necessities like toy boys was just too much for Williams to take.

He sat back in the chair feeling beaten but resigned to the fact that he would have to take the later flight. But at least he was on his way to the airport.

Little did he know that so was I. To catch a flight to Spain.

Chapter 30 - So Close

As Williams' bargain basement flight landed, mine was taking off. Williams had spent most of his flight snoring and consequently disturbing most of the passengers who were trying to watch the inflight film. To be fair to Williams, it was probably a wise move as the little old lady in the next seat was carrying a very strong odour of urine and Tweed and several of the other passengers had asked to be moved.

As Williams was oblivious to the world, I was reclining in my first class seat eating lobster and drinking the airline's finest wine. Part of me was becoming accustomed to all this extravagant living whilst the other part of me missed the simpler things that had always made me happy. But there's a lot to be said for first class travel isn't there?

After a smooth flight, I landed safely at Malaga Airport at three fifteen in the afternoon. As I stepped off the plane the heat hit me. I could smell Spain. You know that smell that wafts in through the coach window as you make your way to your hotel or villa?

I knew that I could never go back to Britain again. The sun and the warmth made you feel alive in a way that grey, cloudy skies could never do.

I flagged down a taxi outside the airport and asked the driver to take me to a nice quiet area by the coast that wouldn't be inundated with tourists.

He took me to a beautiful, little, secluded fishing bay and I sensed that I could live happily there without being tracked down by Williams.

My first priority was to enquire with the locals as to where I could find cheap, but comfortable accommodation and I spent the next few hours walking round the place that was to become my new home.

Unknown to me, Williams was stepping off his plane in the Maldives. He walked through the airport customs wearing a pair of flip flops, a white t-shirt and cut off denim shorts. The only difference between him and a bottle of milk was that he hadclothes on.

He found himself outside the airport and straightaway began to hail a taxi. When the taxi pulled over, Williams got in, sat down and immediately produced a picture from his wallet and then asked the driver:

"Have you seen this woman? She's called Shazza"

"Oh, yes. Of course I know Shazza. I'll take you to Shazza's bar now", the driver said in the local accent.

Williams' face lit up; he couldn't believe his luck.

After a twenty minute drive the taxi pulled up at a bar that had a sandwich board outside with the words "Shazza's Bar" wrote on it in chalk.

Williams paid the taxi driver in the local currency, not knowing how much he had paid for the fare.

He walked into the bar, put down his suitcase, sat down on one of the bar stools, casually took out his sunglasses and put them on his head.

He thought he looked like Steve McQueen whereas in fact he looked more like one of them old men off a saucy postcard from Blackpool. He took out a cigarette and lit it.

The bar man, who had been waiting patiently to take his order, asked Williams what he wanted.

Williams said: "I'll tell you what I want, mate. I want Shazza. Quickly followed by a vodka and coke. Make it a double and don't go too heavy on the coke."

"That'll be four Rufiyaa, please", the bar man said.

"Oh, I don't think so. I think Shazza will be getting this one", Williams replied with a smirk on his face.

The next second the bar man walked towards the rear of the bar area, stuck his head through a beaded curtain, and shouted: "Shazza, there's a man here says he wants you and he's just said you'll pay for his double vodka and coke."

Before the bar man had finished what he was saying a woman walked through the beaded curtain. She must have been thirty stone with more tattoos than Williams and Popeye put together (and they were spelt right!). She smiled at Williams. "Oh, yes love, I'll get these. But what are you going to do for me big boy?"

Williams' face went red and he hastily said: " I think there's been a mistake!"

"Oh, I don't think so. I think it's my lucky day," the woman said, with the biggest smile on her face.

She'd thought her lottery ticket had come up. With all six numbers!

Williams, still amazed at the woman's likeness to Pat Wickes, picked up his suitcase, hastily drank the double vodka and told her, "I'll just go and freshen up and I'll be back tonight. Don't be late!" and he made a hasty escape out of the bar.

He promptly jumped into a taxi and not one to be put off he produced the picture yet again. "Excuse me, mate. Do you know Shazza? And I don't mean the Shazza who owns that bar," Williams shouted at the taxi driver.

"Oh, yes. I know Shazza. She runs a little hotel down the road. I take you to it," the driver said enthusiastically.

Williams was so focussed on getting to the hotel that he didn't notice his beautiful surroundings as he was still a little unnerved by his narrow escape with the owner of Shazza's bar.

The taxi arrived at a small hotel in a quiet, palm tree lined street. Williams left his suitcase inside the taxi and asked the driver to wait for him while he just ran in to check he had got the right place.

Williams went into the hotel and immediately showed the receptionist the photograph and asked, " Do you know this lady? She's called Shazza. Well I say lady, she's no lady really, I believe she runs this hotel. Can you get her for me please?"

"I'm sorry sir, the woman who runs this hotel is 86. She moved over from England forty years ago. So I don't think it's her," the young lady behind the desk said.

At this moment Williams realised he had been done over by the little Maldivian taxi driver. He ran out of the hotel quickly only to see the car driving away with his gear still in the back. There was about two feet difference between Williams and the taxi driver so all Williams could assume was that the little man would have his gear on Ebay quicker than he could say ,"you've been done, mate!" He wasn't having a good day. As usual.

He decided to take a walk along the beach front, calm his nerves and try to replace some of his missing clothes. He had been walking along the street for a couple of minutes when all of a sudden his attention was caught by a shop front that sold designer handbags. He thought it was worth a try.

He went inside and smiled at the assistant who was stood behind the glass fronted counter. Now Williams wasn't the sharpest tool in the box but he had twigged that if he mentioned the name Shazza to any local then they were going to say they knew her and lead him down the garden path for the equivalent of a few quid. He decided to change his tactics.

"Hello, love. You don't know this woman do you? " Williams asked.

"Oh, yes! That's Shazza. She's our best customer. She bought our most expensive bag last week. The commission I got from that sale paid my rent for a month. She's very generous as well. Gave me a very nice tip", the young girl replied.

"Oh, I fuckin' bet she did. You don't know where she's staying by any chance do you?" Williams asked her.

"Oh, yes. I do actually. She goes to the same bar as I do. She's very generous there too. Bought me pina coladas all night last week. Said she'd come into some money. Mentioned an inheritance or something," the girl said in response to Williams' enquiry.

"Oh, really! Was it some old bag ....who died? " Williams asked the girl.

"She did mention a bag funnily enough", the girl added and started to write an address down on a piece of paper that lay on the top of the counter.

Williams at long last now had a lead. It had taken him long enough. He was definitely no Morse, that's for sure. He was in a state of shock that his thirty grand was being enjoyed by the inhabitants of the island.

He caught a taxi to the address on the paper and when he finally arrived he got out, paid the taxi driver and entered the bar.

Williams spotted a rather virile looking young man stood behind the bar throwing a cocktail shaker in the air and he knew immediately why I had made the place my regular watering hole over the last few weeks. Yes, that's right. Because the young man in front of him was a very good bar tender.

Williams thought he was only minutes away from finding me and the remnants of his money.

"Hiya, mate. Do you know this lady and could you tell me what time she comes in please?" Williams asked.

"Oh, yes I know her. That's Shazza. She's very generous. Always gives me a big tip. She's just left to go to Spain to see an old aunt or something," he answered.

"When did she go mate?" Williams asked him.

"Oh, you've just missed her. She left this morning mentioning Malaga and buying more handbags," the young man replied.

Williams knew he had just made a wasted journey but at least he had a lead. Worried that there would soon be no money left, he made his way (minus his luggage) to the nearest taxi rank in order to get back to the airport.

He arrived twenty minutes later, walked straight to the enquiries desk and said: "One way to Manchester please and pronto!"

Twelve hours later, after having bought eight pints and four packets of extortionately priced
sandwiches, Williams was on Flight 454 back to Manchester. His pocket £856 lighter and still no nearer to finding me or his ever dwindling thirty grand.

Having spent a couple days in the most beautiful and tranquil fisherman's cottage, I began to feel safe and relaxed in my new home. The rent was affordable and it had the most beautiful view which overlooked the bay.

On the third day I decided that, if I kept a low profile, it would be okay to venture into the more cosmopolitan areas of Malaga.

It was hot and the sky was an azure blue and again I realised that I was meant for better climes than those of Salford.

I walked round the shops stopping myself from spending any more money as I had come to the conclusion that Williams' money was not going to last forever and I needed to get a job and start a new life here.

I had spent quite a lot of Williams' money on luxuries like designer handbags and perfume and some of it on necessities like alcohol so I had to start being more careful as to how I was spending my money.

Despite the fact that I felt much better in warmer climates, I knew I could never go back because Williams would never forgive me for taking his money. He might forgive me for leaving him standing at the altar but not for taking his thirty grand. For all I knew he could have been hot on the trail.

I walked down one of the back streets admiring the whitewashed taverns and houses that had bright red geraniums in terracotta pots outside every door. It looked just like one of the posters you see in your local travel agents. I loved the place and pictured myself staying there forever.

All of a sudden, I spotted a sign in a tavern window.

The tavern had a traditional British pub sign outside with a picture of a mitre and the words "Pope's Bar" underneath it.

The irony of the tavern's name was not lost on me as I remembered my short lived relationship with DCI Pope who had used me just to find out much sought after information about Williams' escapades.

The sign read: Barmaid Wanted: Apply Within.

It was just what I needed so I walked in with every intention of applying for the job. It would tide me over for the time being and give me some sort of stability for the foreseeable future.

As I entered the bar I noticed a man behind the bar who was filling the shelves with lager bottles. I noticed that he had quite a well-toned muscular build.

I coughed to catch his attention. "Excuse me, I'm just enquiring about the job advertised in your window."

The man turned round and as our eyes made contact I felt myself starting to shake. It was him.

No, not Williams. It was DCI Pope. The man who Williams had conned into thinking there was a stash of money buried in his mam's back garden. Pope had spent three days digging up Mrs Williams' garden (along with his GMP colleagues) to find nothing. The dig did not prove pointless however as two weeks later Mrs Williams had a brand new raised patio.

The meeting with Pope felt uncomfortable as when I had last seen him I had been with Williams who had humiliated him by mentioning his demotion to the job of patrolling a notorious council estate on a rusty Raleigh bike.

"Sharon, is that you?" Pope asked me.

"Yes, Jonathan. It's me", I answered. I had always called him Jonathan whenever I had met him. The only man I called by his surname was Williams. It had always felt right to call him

Williams. It always sounded funny; and that's what our friendship was based on; having fun. Jonathan was different. I fell for his charm. But it had all been an act.

He had only been charming to make me fall for him so that I would give him details about Williams' illegal dealings.

"What are you doing here?" he asked me.

"You know that stash you spent three days looking for in Williams' mam's garden? Well, I didn't have to spend quite so long looking for it. Took me two minutes to find it. Just had a lovely fortnight in the Maldives and now I'm here. Anyway, what are you doing here, Jonathan?"

"Well Sharon, because of Williams and his antics, life was becoming unbearable on Brook House estate. I was being abused by kids asking me if I had found any treasure and taking the mick out of my bike. I just had to get away from it all. It all got too much. So I took redundancy and it was enough to come out here and buy this place. I only have a little mortgage for twenty thousand so I can make a nice living," he said.

I felt a little sorry for him as I imagined him riding around on a little bike ringing his bell.

"Did you really take his money, Sharon?" he asked me.

"Yes, I wanted to get away, Jonathan. I needed a new start," I answered him.

"Sharon, I never meant to hurt you. I had to do it to find out about Williams. I was under orders. I really did like you, you know," he added, appearing genuine.

"Really? I didn't know, Jonathan," I said, choosing to believe him straightaway. His big brown eyes made him look like doe eyed and vulnerable.

"Yes, Sharon, really," he said.

My heart suddenly felt like plasticine being moulded and played with and I didn't know what to say. I needed to stay calm so I asked him: " So can I apply for the job, Jonathan?"

"You don't need to apply. The job's yours."

His voice sounded silky smooth and all of a sudden I needed a drink.

"If you're sure. When do you want me start? I'll try and find somewhere nearer to live," I said trying to appear calm and collected but aware that I must have appeared flustered. "Sharon, you can move in here. There's a room upstairs and it'll save you paying rent. I could do with company to be honest. All that malarkey with Williams played havoc with my self-esteem."

I showed him my gratitude and told him I would bring my belongings the day after and I would start the next night.

Two days later we working together behind the bar and I felt safe and fairly content that I was making a new life.

By the third day I had seen another side to Jonathan Pope. Out of a police uniform he seemed almost human. That afternoon he took me to a local bullfight and we sat in the crowd and entered into the spirit of things. He made a joke about how he could see Williams having a go at being a matador and how he wished that the bull would pin him up against the hoardings with its horns.

We both laughed. Jonathan was out here starting to rebuild his life and so was I. We were two lost souls and it was a perfect match.

On the fourth day I thought I would try to help him out and said: "Look, Jonathan. If you want I can go in with you on the bar and you won't have any mortgage then. No strings attached; it's a genuine offer," I said.

"Sharon, what a good idea. Let's make it official. You come in with me, you have a third ownership and I tell you what, let's get engaged," Jonathan said.

I couldn't believe my ears. Without hesitating I said yes. I would have been stupid to turn down the chance of part owning of a bar in a warm and welcoming country wouldn't I?

Things were looking up for me.

Williams had arrived back in England feeling frustrated and wondering what to do next. He wasn't going to let the failed trip to the Maldives beat him. Once he had the bit between his teeth he wouldn't let go.

He had put the word out that he needed some work in Spain and within days he received a phone call saying that some money needed laundering. He was told to go and visit the Johnson boys (dad and lad) who were, fortunately for Williams, based in Malaga.

Williams couldn't believe his luck. He knew within hours of landing that he would know exactly where I was. He packed his bag full of bent money (he didn't have a suitcase; it was being used as pig trough on a farm in the Maldives) and he booked the next available flight to Malaga airport.

On arrival he was met by Newton le Willows' finest, Graham Johnson.

Williams smiled for the first time in weeks as he was met by his old friend. "Alright, Jonno. How's things, mate?" Williams asked.

"Sound, mate. Couldn't be better", Johnson replied before adding: "Let me carry that bag, mate. Must be heavy!"

They both laughed and made their way to Johnson's villa. When they arrived there they were met by Johnson's son, Scott, who was busy washing his brand new Range Rover Sport which had been picked up that morning straight out of the showroom.

Williams was taken to a luxurious room that had been prepared especially for his arrival and Johnson said to him:

"Make yourself at home, mate. I think you might need a good rest. I believe you got stood up at the altar. What happened?"

"Tricky cow took my money from under the bed so I've come here looking for her. Shazza's her name. Cheeky bitch went to the Maldives splashing the cash, treating all the bloody locals to drinks all night on my money!" Williams answered.

"You're joking aren't you? I know where she is. Someone told me about her the other week," replied Johnson.

"She's with that ex cop Pope," said young Scott. "He's got a bar over here in one of the back Streets."

"Really?" shrieked Williams, amazed at his luck at finding me so quickly. He had anticipated days, if not weeks, of putting the feelers out in order to find me. He felt optimistic that it wouldn't be long before he was back in possession of his money. It was at this point that an old lady appeared at the door carrying a tray.

"Sandwiches, lads," she said. "You must be famished after that flight, especially carrying that heavy bag. Get a brew down you," she added, winking at Williams.

"Thanks, Aunty Pat," the boys replied smiling at the old lady who they obviously adored.

"Is that Pope the one you had digging your mam's garden up?" Scott asked.

"Yea, that's the one, mate", Williams replied. "The pair of them are not going to believe it when I turn up at the bar," he added.

"Don't go rushing in too quick, mate. Let's just sit down and think it through. It won't be hard to come up with something to sort that pillock out!" Johnson senior said.

As the champagne flowed celebrating Williams' arrival they discussed several plans which all involved Pope suffering as they all disliked him as much as he disliked Williams.

The plan they came up with was for Williams to make

friends with me and Pope and appear to have let bygones be bygones.

Williams agreed it sounded like a good plan, they agreed on their plan and Williams retired to bed that night smiling menacingly.

Three days later Williams no longer resembled a milk bottle after sitting around the Johnson's pool and he decided it was time to pay a visit to Pope's bar.

Williams made his way through the streets and eventually found the tavern.

He walked up to the bar and said: "Hello, Pope. Hello Shazza".

Pope's face was a picture and so was mine.

Williams said: "What a surprise! My two old school friends."

"Look Williams, we don't want any trouble. We're a couple now and we're both here to forget about the past," Jonathan responded.

"That's easy for you to say. I'm thirty grand out of pocket and was made to look a right pillock on my wedding day! How do you two suggest we sort it out?" Williams asked us, as we stood there stunned at his sudden appearance.

"Williams, I haven't got any of your money left. I gave it to Jonathan to pay off the rest of the mortgage on this place", I said trying to appeal to his better nature.

"Well, I suppose that makes me part owner of this bar then" Williams delivered his sucker punch.

"Prove it!" I goaded him.

"Oh, so we want to go down that road, do we Shazza?" he asked me.

Jonathan jumped in quick, "Look, I told you we don't want any trouble".

"That's ok, neither do I. But how do you suggest you pay

me back?" Williams asked us.

"Let us think about it. Come back tomorrow and we'll have thought of something by then," Jonathan said.

He left the bar disappearing into the street. The pair of us deflated but trying to think of something to pacify a clearly disgruntled Williams.

The next day WIlliams came into the bar and put a suggestion forward to the pair of us. Jonathan was uncomfortable with the thought of doing anything that wasn't kosher. He had never done anything that was dodgy in his life and was dreading what the suggestion was going to be.

We listened to Williams and reluctantly agreed to his suggestion knowing that it would be the only way we would be free of him.

The next morning we went to the bank and Jonathan withdraw the remnants of his account that he had been intending to use on doing the bar up. I had five grand left so two hours later Jonathan nervously handed over the twenty thousand to Williams. We weren't happy at losing the money but as we watched Williams leave the bar we thought it was worth it to see him disappear from our lives.

Williams arrived back at his host's villa and said to the father and son:

"He's fell for it again!"

All of the next week Williams went no further than the edge of the Johnson's swimming pool and the twenty thousand lay untouched in the bottom of his bag.

Thinking he had returned to Salford, we felt a sense of relief that he was gone and to be honest it was worth handing over the money just to get rid of him.

Chapter 33 - The Flower Seller

The next few weeks Jonathan and myself spent the days and nights working in the bar whilst any spare time we had was spent taking walks on the beach, hand in hand, or walking through the town looking for cheap nick nacks to make our little room above the tavern more homely.

The bar had started to do really well and we were making a profit of around three hundred pounds a night. We were getting on together and I no longer thought of Jonathan as DCI Pope. He was now just a bar owner in Spain.

It would never be the same as it was with Williams but it had taken Williams too long to realise what he had in me and he'd never be reliable. But he had made me tougher and resilient and taught me how to get by without anybody's help; I can't dispute that. And although Jonathan may not make me feel as warm as toast inside like Williams did, at least I knew where I stood with Jonathan.

We'd not heard a peep out of Williams. He'd made me happy in the past but I needed to forget about him and that was exactly what I was doing.

By the end of the third week we were upbeat; the profits from the bar confirmed to Jonathan that it had been a good investment.

We had lots of British customers who always commented on how welcome we made them feel and that Jonathan was a gentleman.

I imagined what Williams would have been like if he was running the bar. No doubt he would have been effing and jeffing and offending the punters left, right and centre. Part of me thought he would be a nightmare and part of me smiled because I could imagine that the customers would love him too. Not because he was a gentleman but because he made them realise that life was for living.

The next week we decided that we would go for a walk round the less touristy parts of the town and try and find a few bits to start making a real home out of the living quarters of the tavern. We looked in half a dozen shops until we found one that we liked.

After half an hour of browsing we had purchased a locally made rug, a rickety old cane chair and a bright red clay vase.

We sat outside a bar and had a few lagers. They were ice chilled and tasted refreshing. The sun was shining, the sky was clear and the world looked good. Things were definitely starting to look up.

When we had finished our drinks, we set off to go back to the tavern. We walked through a busy square that was alive with traders and tourists when suddenly an old lady came up to us selling flowers. She hadn't many left so I assumed that she was selling them for a fair price.

"Hello, lovey. Would you like some flowers for that er....interesting vase?" the lady said to me. "How much are they?" I asked her.

"I tell you what, cos you're a fellow Brit I'll let you have them for 2 Euros. They'll last at least a week. There's some of that crystal flower food in that packet. Just put them in the water and you'll get an extra two days out of them. Makes them nice and perky, love", she smiled looking at Jonathan and give him a wink as she said the word perky.

I liked her, and she had a Northern accent, so I paid her the two Euros and took the flowers from her and said thank you.

We got back to the tavern and went straight upstairs to the living area. I put the rug down and placed the cane chair near the window, filled the vase with water, poured the crystallised food in it and placed the flowers inside. I put the vase on a small table that was placed in the middle of the room and stepped back to look at our newly dressed living quarters.

It was beginning to look like a home. I sat in the cane chair, looked out of the window at the beautiful view and sighed. I was happy. I could quite easily stay here I thought.

We went to bed that night feeling a sense of security and contentment. But at three o'clock in the middle of the night that sense of security was shattered when we heard a banging on the door downstairs.

We ran down and opened the door to be met by three local police.

"Can we step inside and search the premises please?"one of them asked.

"Look, I'm an ex Detective Constable and I assure you I have never done anything illegal in my life. Which is unusual for a copper I know, but I can promise you, you'll find nothing in here," Jonathan told him.

"Well, if you don't mind wc'll take a look anyway," the policeman replied, pushing past us and heading towards the stairs.

We followed all three policemen upstairs and watched them search systematically through every single object we had in the room.

Suddenly, the quieter member of the three policemen said: "Found something, sir".

He had drained the water from the vase and there, on the sink, were ten sparkling diamonds. Now I know nothing about diamonds but they were shiny and beautiful and I assumed they were worth a few bob. I was not fully awake but suddenly I knew that I had to think on my feet. Williams had taught me that, so I looked at Jonathan and said:

"Oh, no. What have you done...now?"

Jonathan was handcuffed to one of the policemen and led out to a waiting car. I remained at the tavern, contemplating my next move.

Chapter 34 - Do Unto Others

Back in Salford, Williams' phone rang at five in the morning that very same day.

"You owe Aunty Pat a drink mate, and make it a big 'un! And if you want to come and stay here while the trial's going on you're very welcome," Johnson's voice said.

"Nice one, mate. So it worked then? Knew we'd get the bastard. I'll be on the next plane available. Tell Aunty Pat thanks very much and I'll be getting her a very big drink", Williams said.

Williams' plane touched down the next day. His face was very different from the last time he had been in Malaga. This time he was grinning from ear to ear. He had recovered two thirds of the money I had taken and he had got the better of Pope yet again.

Jonathan's arrest was the talk of the town. All anyone could talk about was 'that nice Englishman who ran Pope's Bar.' How could a pillar of society like that be involved in a diamond theft? Especially an ex copper. And to make matters worse the diamonds had been stolen from the local mayor's personal collection.

The fact that the mayor had got them through ill gotten gains was irrelevant but Williams, the Jonno boys and Aunty Pat, all knew how they had come to be in that vase in the first place.

After speaking to some of the regulars who came into the bar, I phoned the British Consul for advice. They already knew about Jonathan's arrest and had set the wheels in motion to get him an excellent solicitor.

The fact that he was an ex policeman was to his advantage.

I was told that he was to appear in court the next morning on the charge of the theft of diamonds worth a quarter of a million pounds.

I arrived at the local court at ten thirty the next morning. I took my place in the court room awaiting to see what was going to happen to him. I was just thankful that my name had not been involved in the whole thing. I was astonished that I had not been interviewed but was grateful nevertheless.

The judge entered the room; he had a look of Antonio Banderas which made the prospect of spending the next few hours in a stuffy court room quite appealing.

The judge was followed by someone I recognised as being the local mayor. I had seen his face in the local paper opening a new wing of the nearby hospital and knew him straightaway.

They were closely followed by Williams, two men who I did not recognise and a woman who looked vaguely familiar.

Suddenly I realised where I had seen her before; she was the lady who had sold me the flowers the day earlier. What was she doing here?

The court room filled up steadily and soon there was not a seat to be had.

When the court room doors were shut the judge said: "The court can now sit down please."

The judge explained to the court what would happen during the proceedings of Jonathan's trial and when he had finished he finally got to the part I had been dreading. I still wasn't entirely sure whether Jonathan was involved or not.

I felt very uneasy after catching sight of Williams with the two other men and wondered how he had come to know about the arrest. Mind you, it was a small town and everyone knew everyone's business.

"How do you plead, Mr Pope?" the judge asked Jonathan.

"Not guilty", Jonathan replied to the judge's question.

My instincts were right and Jonathan denied any wrong

doing.

The proceedings started and for the next few hours I absorbed my surroundings and tried to take in what was happening. To be honest it got a bit boring after the first hour so I began to people watch.

I was fascinated by the old lady who had sold me the flowers and I watched her intently. I was still puzzled as to why she was there but I was to find out why later.

In the second hour the old woman opened the large bag she had placed on her lap and took out a large silver foiled package. She opened it, not caring about the disturbance she was causing with the rustling noise of the aluminium, and started to eat one of the sandwiches inside it.

Part of me wanted to laugh.

Then when she took out a flask with the words "Keep calm and have a brew," embossed on it

I smiled. She must be bored shitless to want to come here and watch this all day, I thought. The whole court room could hear her munching and slurping her tea but to be honest it did add a little interest to the whole proceedings which had become exceedingly dull.

All the evidence pointed towards Jonathan's involvement. There was no disputing that. The prosecuting lawyer had put a very good case forward; even I believed he was guilty. It was only when the judge came back into the court room after retiring to consider his verdict that the seriousness of all this started to hit me.

If he got found guilty how was I going to manage to run the bar by myself? How would I manage on my own? After a few minutes of asking myself, I came to the conclusion that I would manage very well, thank you.

It was probably going to be better and easier doing it without a man's help. And what's more......it would be my bar. I would see a solicitor and get it sorted so that it belonged solely to me. I would find the money somehow. I'd have to get that sign took down tomorrow; that was my first priority.

I started to go through some possible names for the bar. Buried Treasure maybe? Northern Pints? I suddenly stopped day dreaming and started to concentrate on the proceedings when the judge said he was about to announce his verdict.

"Mr Pope, after listening to all the evidence and considering the prosecution's and the defence's cases, I have decided to announce a guilty verdict," the judge said.

The court room was silent. I'm wasn't sure if it was my imagination but I thought I heard humming coming from where Williams' was sat. It sounded vaguely familiar.

It got a little louder then suddenly I heard Williams and the two men singing 'You're going down, you're going down, PC Pope, you're going down' to the tune of Yellow Submarine.

The feud between Williams and Pope had not ended and Williams had had the last laugh. Again. Then, when I seen Williams kiss the old lady on her cheek, it suddenly dawned on me who she was and her connection to Williams.

I should have known. The whole thing smacked of Williams' work. I didn't know what to think anymore. Whenever I seen Williams I didn't know what to think. I didn't know how I felt anymore.

"Mr Pope, You will serve ten years in a Spanish jail for your crimes," the judge said sternly.

Jonathan was led away screaming whilst protesting his innocence.

"It was her over there", Jonathan said pointing to the old lady who was just finishing screwing the lid back on her thermos flask.

He disappeared from view and I slowly made my way to the courtroom exit.

Williams approached me and said: "Shazza, we're going for a celebratory drink. Would you like to join us? There's a few things I need to tell you".

I duly accepted, eager to know what he had to say, and followed him out

Chapter 35 - The Truth

I know what you're thinking as you read this. I know you're shocked at my actions. I can hear you ask how I could walk away from that courtroom after seeing Jonathan sentenced to ten years and calmly go and have a drink with the people who had framed him.

The answer is: quite easily, actually. I had just found myself in possession of a thriving business in the sun with my own place to live and for once the only thing I was worried about was what the man staring at me was going to say.

I would be lying if I said I wasn't scared.

Williams had let me off for ten grand and after seeing the lengths he had gone to in order to get Jonathan jailed I wasn't entirely convinced that he was just going to let me off scot free.

"Shazza, it's not about the money you stole, cos I did tell you to take what you needed but it was the thought of being dragged around all those wedding fayres. I'm still having nightmares now about it. After spending all that money, I just didn't expect you to not turn up on our wedding day. I honestly thought with all my heart that you loved me. Can you imagine how I felt having to tell all our guests that you'd done one to the Maldives? You made me look a right bloody idiot. And now I want some answers", Williams said to me.

He was calm but never the less I was still anxious as to where the conversation was going to lead.

"Oh, Williams. You knew that you were the best mate I ever had and you know I love you, but you were only going to marry me because you thought it was the next step in the friendship. You wouldn't have meant what you said if you'd have taken those vows, mate. I would always have been second best. You never wanted to ravage me mate did you? You would have only have wanted me to do your ironing and clean your toilet. If you were honest you would say "Yes, Shazza, You're right."

"That's why I took it, mate. For a fresh start. And you taught me all I know. It wasn't a patch on the buried treasure hoax or the diamonds but it was pretty good wasn't it, mate?"

"But you made me look a right knob, Shazza, having to tell everybody. Then having to sell all them presents on Ebay , then having to bump loans left right and centre to get to the Maldives. Then, I hear you're spending all my till buying drinks for the locals. Still, at least I travelled a bit and yes, I can understand why you did it. I just needed to hear you tell me why", he said.

I had never seen him looking so serious. I decided it was time to tell him how he had made me feel. "Williams, mate. You know that day at your daughter's wedding? When everyone was looking at you going down on one knee in front of me making them all think you were going to propose and then you made a joke that you'd torn a cartilage. You humiliated me in front of 300 guests. I wanted you to know how I felt that day. So I hope you did what I did the same as me, mate. And that was just smile, keep your dignity, get drunk and get on with it," I answered him.

"Bollocks to my dignity, that went at the altar. All them bloody guests, Shazza. Had to go up to every single one of them and say the same thing over and over again. All the time you were on the plane laughing at me. The thing is Shazza, they were all my mates that I had to explain it all to. All your friends just took the bloody flowers from the church and pissed off. The worst part was that most of my mates said you were too good for me and they didn't blame you for not turning up", Williams said.

"Well, they're not all wrong are they?" I said, not being able to stop myself. It was him who had taught me to be hard and tough but now he didn't like it.

"Oh, look how the worm's turned, now she's got a bit of sun on her back!", he said jokingly.

I sensed that he was mellowing and the answers I had given him may have satisfied his curiosity as to why I had done it. But I realised that it had been morally wrong to take the money and hesitatingly, I offered him the money back.

"Look, I know it was wrong. I will pay you back as soon as I can. The bar's doing well so it shouldn't take me long". I said, regretting my offer as soon as I had said it.

"Look, mate. It's not about the money, perhaps you're right. I did need a lesson like that teaching to me. So this is what I'm prepared to do. Most of what you've told me is right. And it probably would have ended up a disaster. So, we'll forget about the money because you know I care about you and I always will. You've taught me to respect people and things and you taught me how to love again. That in itself is worth more than any money you owe me. But all I ask, is that, whenever I come over to see the Jonno boys, I will be made welcome in your bar. But, Shazza, I suggest you change its name," Williams had said all this as though he had been thinking through what he was going to say like a Bafta winner learning his lines for his acceptance speech.

"Mate, I will change the name of the bar tomorrow. I'm going to call it The Worm has Turned. Do you like it, mate?", I asked him.

"Yes, Shazza. I like it," he smiled. "Can I ask you what you're going to do about that knobhead?" he added.
"Well, mate. I think considering he got himself involved in a major diamond theft, it may be best to distance myself from him. After all, I don't want to be fraternising with dodgy people do I? I think that bar will be a little goldmine and it's mine now. That's all I need. But its doors are always open for you, you know that,"

I said, meaning every single word.

"That's good of you, Shazza. Here's the number for the Jonno boys; they'll keep their eyes out for you. I wish you lots of luck in your new business. But I've got to go home to Salford now Pope's not on the scene and Shazza, it's too hot over here for me. I couldn't stand it," Williams said.

"I appreciate that. You'll always be welcome and we'll always be mates. I'm really glad I went to that school reunion and met you. That night really did change my life and for the better," I said to him, thinking back to the very first time I met him.

Williams looked me in the eyes and kissed me like he'd never done before.

Bit bloody late now, I thought. And with that he left the bar and said goodbye. But my instincts told me I might be hearing from him in the not too distant future.

Williams was on the next flight to Manchester and I was left wondering what could have been.

Williams flight landed back at Manchester at six thirty in the morning. He went through customs with five times the allowed amount of duty free. He had enough ciggies and vodka to last him all of four days.

He got a taxi and headed straight to his mam's house. He paid the taxi driver the exact fare, picked up his case and walked to wards the front door of Mrs Williams' house. He knocked on the door and his mam opened the door smiling as she recognised her son stood on her front doorstep.

"Hiya, Simon. You look brown love," she said.

"Sun Cabin, Langworthy Road, mam. £1 for three minutes and they've only just put new tubes in as well" , he said, before asking her: " What have you been up to, mam?"

"Just sat out on the patio, love. Do you know it gets the sun all day now them lovely boys in blue have moved it a couple of feet. I've missed you son, where have you been?" Mrs Williams asked.

"Oh, I've been about doing this and that, mam. I've been offered redundancy so I think I'll take it. I should cop for a few bob. So I've decided to do my house up. Do a bit of a makeover. Have you still got that Lowry that I gave you years ago? " he asked.

"Yes, course I have son. Why? Would you like it back? " she asked.

"Yes, if you don't mind. I've got big plans for that," he said.

"Where are you going to put it? Over the fireplace?", Williams' mam asked.

"Yea, something like that, mam", he answered.

"Here's some money towards your bills mam, I know you don't get much on a pension", he offered her, pulling a wad of folded up notes from his back pocket.

"There's too much there son," she said, embarrassed at his generosity.

"No, mam. I insist. I've got a feeling my luck's really going to change for the better.

"Have you heard from that Shazza, son?" she asked, "I liked her, she was a good girl."

"I know mam, I just couldn't see what was under my nose until it was too late. By the time I was going to marry her she'd had enough. Anyway, I heard she's got a bar now in Spain," he said.

"Oh, has she? You've not got the address have you? I wouldn't mid going over to see her."

"No, I haven't mam, but I could get it. I'm sure she'd make you feel welcome."

With that Williams quickly said his goodbyes and left with the Lowry, holding it securely as if his life depended on it.

On returning home he put the painting on the table, went to the kitchen, pulled out a magnifying glass from out of the drawer and inspected the painting to find the one figure that stood out amongst the hundreds making their way to their daily work in the factory. He found it and then very carefully removed the very lifelike image of a mobile phone that was being held by the matchstick man.

Williams had a painting worth hundreds of thousands of pounds. He smiled to himself, pulled out a piece of paper from his back pocket, walked to the phone and dialled the number written down on it.

"Hello, is that Sotheby's? Yes, I'd like to place an item in the next auction please. What is it? It's a Lowry, mate. Salford's finest", he said to the man on the other end of the line.

"Has the painting got a title please?" the man enquired.

"Yes, mate. The Factory Gates,1938", Williams replied.

"Oh, I believe that painting was lost some years ago, sir", the man said.

"Oh, no. I don't think so, mate. It's been on my wall for donkeys years", Williams assured him.

The man seemed very excited at the prospect of a Lowry original being offered to his auction house. "We'll send the specialists to pick it up if you're happy to have us deal with it for you, sir", the man said eagerly thinking about his commission.

"Not a problem", said Williams.

"OK, sir. We'll have someone pick it up in the next five hours", the man said.

"If you want to phone me when you arrive in Salford I'll direct you", Williams said giving the man his mobile number.

Williams said goodbye to the man at the other end of the phone rubbed his hands and started to smile. It was not just a smile it was an enormous grin that stretched from ear to ear.

Williams was excited as he travelled to London, hoping to get a good result with the Lowry. Having parked in a multi-story in the centre of London, Williams made his way across the busy city to Sotheby's auction house.

He entered the famous building and made his way to the room listed inside the auction leaflet that had been sent to him earlier in the week. There, on page one of the booklet, was his Lowry.

There was a photograph of it and a description followed by a guide price of a hundred thousand pound.

Williams could not believe his luck.

Days before he had been looking at houses in the Lancaster Road area of Salford. He had seen a house that needed some renovation work doing and a bit of money spending on it and he had thought that it could be the one for him; his castle.

He took his seat and the auctioneer introduced himself:

"Good afternoon, ladies and gentlemen. My name is Joshua Condron and I'd like to thank you all for coming to Sotheby's today and wish you all a good day. We have some very interesting lots in the sale today so happy bidding."

The first few lots were sold for less than expected and Williams started to wonder if he should set his sights a little lower than Lancaster Road. Maybe, he thought, he should consider going back to his childhood hunting ground of Langworthy Road.

But, then, on reflection, he thought that maybe it wouldn't be such a bad thing. After all, it's the people that make a place and the people of Langworthy were the salt of the earth in

Williams' eyes.

Suddenly his thoughts were interrupted by the auctioneer announcing the sale of a 1938 Lowry entitled 'The Factory Gates'. He then informed the bidders that he had commission bids starting at two hundred and fifty thousand pounds.

Williams nearly fell off his chair. Within five minutes the bidding had reached four hundred and seventy five thousand pounds. Williams was in a state of shock; he could not believe his luck and was practically hyperventilating.

The hammer finally went down at five hundred and twenty thousand pounds. The auction room started clapping. Williams knew the very instant the hammer fell that, like mine, his life would be changed forever.

Chapter 38 - Happy Days

Williams was in a state of bewilderment as he drove home. The thought of having so much money confused him and he didn't know what to do first. First of all he splashed out on twenty Sterling Superkings instead of the usual ten.

Different thoughts were going through his mind and it took several days for these thoughts to subside until he decided what he was going to do with his windfall.

After the sale was officially confirmed and the cheque had cleared, the very first thing he did was to give his children fifty thousand pounds each.

He then went to the estate agents and paid cash for the house he had seen on Lancaster Road, even having the cheek to get the asking price reduced by five thousand pounds.

He then took a cutting out of the Salford City Reporter that mentioned the sale of the Lowry. It commented on the fact that the Lowry had mysteriously turned up for auction at Sotheby's auction house in London and had sold for an astonishing amount of money.

He then proceeded to find all his old Marvel comics (the ones with Wonder Man in) and after finding them in his loft, he sat down and started to write a letter.

Dear Shazza,

Hope you're okay mate. You're never going to believe what's happened to me! I've sold that Lowry for half a million quid. It only turned out to be an original. I had no idea! I've been able to treat my kids like I've always wanted to and I've bought myself a place on Lancaster Road, so next time you come home, you've always got a place to stay.

My mam and her sister, Anne, are on their way over to your place, so enclosed is a cheque for twenty grand. It's what's left over from the half a million; I thought you deserved it for showing me what's right and wrong in life. While my mam and Aunty Anne are with you make sure they don't have to put their hands in their purse.

Be a love and send your mate Pope the enclosed cuttings and these Wonder Man comics and let him know that I've just bought a brand new Audi TT and it's all mine; not the GMP's. For once in my life I can explain where I've got the money from. Well, sort of.

Shazza, is there any chance I can come over and stay at yours if it ever comes out over here?

Love always, Williams x

I received that letter two days ago about two hours before Mrs Williams and her sister arrived.

They settled in very quickly. And I have to tell you, that last night was one of the most eventful since I had owned the bar. Mrs Williams and Aunty Anne, sang on the Karaoke until three in the morning. Their rendition of Stayin' Alive kept the punters in their seats until the early hours and the takings were double what they normally were. By the end of the evening everyone (including all the locals, the village mayor and the Jonno boys) was singing Matchstick Men and Matchstick Cats and Dogs at the top of their voices. In fact, many of the locals asked could the two sisters become a regular turn on a Friday night.

The atmosphere was fantastic and I realised my future was here; making people happy through drink and welcoming arms. The singing could be heard throughout the village and rumour has it could even be heard in the local village prison.

Rumour also has it that half of the inmates were joining in.

HIDDEN DEPTHS

SALFORD BORN AND BRED

CHAPTER 1 THE DAY AFTER

As I walked into the Civic Centre the day after the night before, I didn't really know what to expect. I was greeted by my secretary, a lovely, nicely dressed in a beige suit, and a well-mannered woman.

"Hi, I am Susan Irving," she said, smiling. "I am looking forward to working with you for the next four years."

"Likewise. First thing's first, though, Susan. Are you a Salford girl?"

"Yes, Mr. Mayor," she stated proudly.

"In which case, Susan, call me Simon. Save the fancy titles for posh doo's."

"Oh, the last mayor was well into them," she replied.

"I know, and now, they stop. I will start as I mean to go on. That means cutting down on all the elaborate parties and civic functions, and concentrate on getting this great city back to its former glory."

She beamed. "That's why I voted for you. I know you will

sort this mess out."

"We had better get started then. I need to see the accounts to figure out why there have been so many cuts."

"Don't worry, Simon, I will get them straight away." She grinned as she left the office. It seemed genuine; a smile that said, 'I know he means what he is saying.' The hard work was just about to begin.

****

I opened the accounts, and started to try and make some sense of them. None of it added up. I buzzed through to Susan telling her I was not to be disturbed, under any circumstances, unless it was Dianne. I was always available for Dianne, in every respect. Because if I wasn't, she'd kill me.

I couldn't believe what I was reading. There was more fiddling going on than in the BBC Philharmonic. The report listed thirteen under-mayors. I rubbed the bridge of my nose, trying to decipher what on Earth was an under-mayor, and why they were costing tax payers a fortune.

You didn't need to be a genius to spot all the welfare cuts to the vulnerable. Home help services had been cancelled, and community transport stopped. Old people's homes were threatened with closure, and childcare provisions had been scrapped. Eight hours, six cups of coffee, and a doughnut later, I realised I couldn't do this alone. I needed help. Figures were never my strong suit, unless they were 36-26-36, of course.

I put a call through to an old accountant friend of mine. "Hello, is that you Julie?"

"Williams. What you up to?" Said Miss Oakley, her voice as cheery as ever.

"Not much, apart from a bit of mayoring."

"Yes, I had heard you were standing for office. Nice to see a Langy Roader come good."

"I know, and right now, I wish I'd paid more attention there. Listen, mate, I need your help and I need it quickly," I explained, trying not to sound too panicky.

"Why, what's up? You don't need bailing out again, Williams, do you?"

"No! Those days are behind me. On the straight and narrow now. Unfortunately, it seems the ex-mayor and his cronies were using the taxpayers' money as a personal bank account. There's money missing here, there, and everywhere. Honestly, Julie, we aren't talking a few quid here. I need to get to the bottom of this. Can you come and see me in the morning, mate?"

"Bloody hell, Williams, you don't want much do you?

"Come on, mate. Help me out. I'm not asking for me. I'm asking for the hard working Salfordians, who have been well and truly shafted by these bandits." Julie had always been a bit of a champion of the people, so I knew she would come through for me.

"Okay, okay. I hope you know it's my manicure and hair day tomorrow, so you owe me, Williams!"

"Okay, mate, don't be late," I replied.

"Cheeky bugger," she laughed.

I had only just put the receiver down when the phone rang. Dianne's dulcet tones filled my ear. "Hey, babe, what time will you be home?"

Just hearing her voice made me feel better. "I'm just finishing up here. Gimme half an hour. It's been a really crappy day, so I might just need one of your special massages and a few voddys to help me unwind."

"Ok. I'll run you a bath and get the baby oil ready. Voddy is already chilling and takeaway ordered."

It was no wonder I loved this girl. *Think I'll keep this one.* I didn't need any more encouragement than that to get me out of the office.

I was greeted at the door with a tender kiss, as always. "So, why was it a crappy day, babe? I thought they would ease you in gently. Long lunch and meeting the staff?

As I told her all about the dodgy deals, missing money, and the poor buggers who were struggling to hold on to their homes, families, and sanity, I realised it sounded like a Charles Dickens story, but without a happy ending. Dianne was so upset, and asked what we could do about it to put thing right.

I told her Julie Oakley was coming over to look at the figures, dropping everything to help me out. I explained all about the mysterious under-mayors and their five figure salaries. "Apart from Susan, my secretary, who seems really quite efficient and a good, honest Salford girl, I don't feel I can trust anyone. Everyone is in somebody's back pocket."

Suddenly, Dianne had one of her brilliant moments of inspiration. "You know what, Si, you could do a lot worse than getting your old mates, Binnsy, Azza and Trotty, on board."

I thought about this for a moment. She was right; I did need good people, one's I could trust with my life. The lads who had always had my back. Why hadn't I thought of it before?

"What are you going to do about the under-mayors?"

Dianne asked.

"I have no option but to let them go. I am going to start at the top and work my way down. Get rid of the hanger's on. At the moment, the only ones who are safe are the cleaners and Susan. The rest will be called in to see me in the next week or so."

Moments later, dinner arrived. It was amazing what a difference a bit of fried rice, a bottle of red, and an all-over massage could make. I slept like a baby for the first time in weeks.

The next morning, I woke early doors, and set off for what I expected was going to be the biggest challenge of my life. Julie arrived promptly at half nine, and began the hard work of going through the books. Poor girl, she had her work cut out for her. I had spoken to Susan first thing, too, and told her to inform all the under-mayors I wanted to see them, one-by-one, at fifteen minute intervals. I asked her to make sure they knew attending was not an option.

I was not sure if it was the stately surroundings of the mayoral office, with its plush green leather chairs and wood panelled walls, or inhaling the polish that went to my head, because I suddenly turned into Lord Sugar, you sir. I was on fire. I banged my fists on the desk, demanding to know how, and why, they had let the people of Salford down so badly. The tirade ended the same every time, without explanation from the offenders. I couldn't help it. I was on a roll. "And that is why you, sir, are fired!" Thirteen times, and it felt better every time.

By the end of the day, I had worked my way through the lot of them. I felt brilliant. Good riddance to bad rubbish, as my mam would say. What I didn't know at the time was I would meet most of them again, under very different circumstances.

After two days of going through the books, Julie told me what I had already guessed. We were short by over six million pounds. That was the easy bit. Now we had to find out where all the money had gone. I could only see two choices. We either got the police in and probably would never see a penny of it again, or do the right thing and get the money back my way. Luckily, I had grown up in Salford, and always knew the right—or some might say the wrong—people.

Only one thing to do if you're a Salford lad. Have a private audience with the under mayors. One by one, go after them for the money they stole. Ok, maybe not the way things should be done but the only way to get things done.

I will never forget the face of a certain under-mayor when confronted by four burly Salford lads, demanding the cash back. Truthfully, I wasn't sure it would work, but it did, without a drop of blood in sight—well, maybe some. Anyway, as a mayor, I couldn't condone violence so we will leave out the details, in case I ever need other offences to be taken into account. Even though we were able to recoup some of the cash, we were still two million pounds off. We had done everything we could, but I knew we had run out of threats. Once again, I turned to Dianne to see if she had any ideas how to move forward, and she suggested I go to Westminster and plead my case for more funding.. My local MP, Tony Flynn, was a good labour man, and helped me all the way with advice on what to say, and what grants to ask for, whom to speak to. With barely two weeks of being the new mayor of Salford, I was off to London, cap in hand…

CHAPTER 2 LONDON CALLING

Dianne packed us both an overnight bag, and we headed off to Victoria Train Station to catch the 12.15 to London Euston. For the first time in our lives, we were travelling first class. Well, it wouldn't be right travelling second class, not for a gentleman in office. I was hoping the trip would be a lot better than the last time we went away together. Dianne still had a pop at me over that, so the less said about it, the better. Though I have to admit, it still made me smile thinking about it.

The train journey to London was surprisingly comfortable, and it had taken us less than three hours. There was a queue of black cabs outside, and we gave the driver of one the name of our accommodation in Westminster. After a short journey, we pulled up outside the very posh hotel. The doorman stepped forward to open the cab door.

"Bloody hell, Williams. Are you sure this is the right place? It's got a red carpet outside!"

"Course I'm sure. No more dodgy B&Bs for us. We are Mr. and Mrs. Lord Mayor now. Only the best for my girl." I grinned, giving her bump a pinch, which she ignored.

The doorman took our bags into the reception area, and turned to us and smiled. "I hope you have a lovely stay with us, Sir." He tipped his hat and stood waiting.

"I hope so, too. Cheers, mate."

The doorman, a little deflated, returned to his post outside.

"You are supposed to give him a tip," said Dianne, giving me a right dig in the ribs. "You don't half show me up sometimes."

"Okay, okay. I'll give him one when we go out later, but right now, I'm knackered, and there's free Sky Sports in the room. Besides, I'm taking you out on the town later, so you'll need a while to get ready."

"Ooh, I love surprises. Where are we going?"

"If I told you, it wouldn't be a surprise, would it?"

We checked in, and headed up to our room. I had ordered champagne for us in advance, and it was on ice, waiting.

"You know, Williams, you're a right old romantic when you want to be, or when you want something in return!"

"Cheeky mare. It's just my way of saying sorry for everything, and saying thank you for standing by me, and helping with the campaign."

Dianne got her glad rags on while I had a kip. I didn't sleep much, even though the bed was very comfortable. I kept having nightmares about standing in front of MPs and trying to get extra funds allocated to our city. I showered and dressed. Though, I say so myself, I looked half decent in my 'court' suit and funeral tie. Finished off with a splash of my new aftershave, Midnight in Monton, I was ready to paint the town red.

We had dinner in a little Italian restaurant, Bella Notte. It was amazing. The food was fantastic, and the wine was going down a treat.

"Right then, Mrs Mayor, time for part two of date night."

We paid the bill and strolled the short distance to the theatre. I slowed down as we approached *The Lion King* posters.

"No way, Williams! Oh my God! We are going to see *The Lion King*? Please tell me we are." I don't think I have ever seen her so happy or excited.

We had great seats in the stalls, with a brilliant view of everything. I wasn't really expecting to enjoy it. Musicals weren't really my thing, but I knew Dianne loves them. Now, if it had been a Smiths' concert...

For the first half of the show, I sat there open mouthed. I was totally blown away. I had never seen anything so incredible. The costumes, the singers, the band. Absobloodylutely amazing. Dianne cried, laughed, and knew all the words to the songs. By the time it finished, I wanted to watch it again. I had forgotten all about the meeting in the morning, and I felt the tension slipping away.

I had one more surprise for Dianne. I waved a cab, and told him our destination. A few minutes later, we were in a pod on the London Eye.

"Who are you? And what have you done with my Simon?" Dianne laughed. "It's so pretty. Thank you." She gently kissed my neck and whispered, "I love you, Williams."

Looking out over London at night was magical. It was a weird feeling glancing over at the brightly lit Houses of Parliament, and thinking how different they would look in the cold light of day.

We decided to walk back to the hotel. Dianne taught me

the words to *Hakuna Matata,* and we sang all the way home. When we got to the hotel, the doorman opened the door for us.

"Cheers, mate. Whisky Galore. 3pm. Newmarket."

While we were waiting for the lift, Dianne asked, "What was all that about? Some sort of code?"

"No. You told me to give him a tip. So, I did"

"Williams, you are awful. Funny, but awful. Thanks for a lovely evening. We should do this more often."

There was more champagne on ice waiting for us in the room. We both slipped on the plush bath robes and slippers laid out neatly on the bed.

"These are coming home with us. My M&S robe isn't as good as this. These are well posh." Dianne glanced back over her shoulder as she went to the bathroom. "So are these toiletries and shower cap. It's all Woods of Windsor stuff, dead expensive in Boots. That ice bucket and champagne flutes can go in my bag, too. Oh, and see if you can find a sewing kit. Posh hotels always have sewing kits."

Evidently, it was true what they say. You could take the girl out of Salford, but you couldn't take Salford out of the girl. Even if she was a school teacher. We only had a couple of glasses of fizz before falling fast asleep.

My alarm went off at seven. I showered, put my suit on, and went down for breakfast. I wasn't really hungry, but I paid for it, so I had to eat it. I made up a breakfast, coffee, and juice, and took Dianne her breakfast in bed. She was already up and showered when I got back so it was breakfast on dressing table not bed. Still, it was the thought that counted.

At half-eight, we set off for my meeting. I really wasn't sure what to expect, but I knew it wasn't going to be easy. At the Houses of Parliament, we were shown into a huge, oak panelled room. There was an enormous, highly polished wooden table, which almost filled the room. The chairs were upholstered in traditional green leather. There were about fifteen of them, and only one was empty: mine.

"Aah, Mr. Williams. Glad you could make it. Please, take a seat."

As soon as I sat down, they started firing questions at me. It was impossible to tell who was from which party, they were all private school, posh boys, trying to catch me out. "Why wasn't I prepared to make cuts?" and "Why do we need food banks?" They were all talking at once, question after question.

I recognised the MP for Chorley, Deborah Hornby. I could hear her voice over all of them. She was one of the expenses scandal MPs, claiming for two houses and £300 a week to pay for a dog walker when she was in London. She had even billed for a new kennel!

"How can you sit here, demanding all this money for these benefit scroungers? Who do you think you are? You're not even an MP!"

Scroungers, hark at the kettle call the pan black. "If you would all just shut up for five minutes, and let me explain everything."

I explained that Salford had had their budget cut, year after year. I explained about the housing problems. I gave them case studies of neglected elderly people, and the lack of funding for police, health and road repairs. Ten, double-sided A4 sheets of all the whys and hows, as well as the pros and cons. I explained the state of affairs the outgoing mayor created. After two hours solid of heated discussions, I summed up. "Look, what I need is a loan. It will be paid back, with interest. Three million will get the city back on track. Please don't write us off. Help me give back the city to the people."

They asked me to step out so they could discuss the fine points. Dianne was waiting in the corridor for me.

"You were ages. How is it going?" she asked

"I'm not sure, to be honest. I'm not hopeful though. That cheating MP from Chorley, Deborah Hornby, was on the panel"

"No! I hope you told her she had no business even being there. She should have been sacked."

"I did. Cheeky cow."

It felt like we had been waiting for hours when they called me back in.

"Well, Mayor Williams, we have decided to give you the loan that you have requested, on the condition it is repaid, with interest, and within a set time frame. We will not make any further austerity cuts this year to give you the opportunity to put things right." When they had finished, I honestly felt like skipping out of there. I was buzzing.

Outside, in the anteroom, Dianne was chatting to an old friend of mine, Tony Flynn, who was also our local MP.

"Alright, mate. How did it go in there? It's a bit like being mauled by lions, isn't it?"

"Nah. Behave, Tony. I had them eating out of the palm of my hand. They don't call me, 'The Charming Man' for naught, you know!"

"No, he pays them," Dianne chipped in.

Tony invited us to have a celebration drink in The Parliament Bar with him later that day.

"Nice thought, Tony," said Dianne, looking disappointed. "Our train home is at six-thirty."

"Hey. Have I taught you nothing, Mrs. Mayor? You never turn down aught for naught. We would love to join you later, Tony."

"Great. See you at six, then. Your day pass will allow you back in."

Tony headed off for Prime Minister's questions, and Dianne and I returned to the hotel.

"We haven't got the room for another night. We can't afford another night, either."

"We can't, you're right. However, we have to go back to the Commons later, so that is business, not pleasure. So, if we have to stay another night here for business, then it's on expenses. They can take it out of the three million quid I just got for them."

"I never thought of it like that," laughed Dianne.

"That's why I am the mayor. You have to think outside the box. Always be one step in front. I think just one more bottle of fizz on the room service bill won't be too much either."

We met Tony at six, as arranged, and true to his word, there was a bottle of Bolly on ice waiting for us. Dianne made me promise not to get drunk and show her up in front of all the toffs. I was in my element, mingling with all the MPs. For the first time, I thought that this mayor business was alright. Posh hotels, great food, free pop, and three million to balance the books. Bloody brilliant!

Six months prior, I had been a labourer, earning a pittance for ten-hour days and zero hours contracts, and now, I was chatting to people I had only ever seen on telly. I didn't know then, but there were even greater changes to come.

"Hey, Dianne. Look over there, near that big pot plant. It's Cuthbert Harrington Potts! He looks like Lord Snooty."

Dianne laughed out loud. "Haha, he does. Oh no. He's coming over."

I had met some slimeballs in my time, but this guy was the worst yet. He totally blanked me, and spoke directly to Dianne's chest. She was desperately trying not to laugh at him because he sounded like Lord Snooty, too. She excused herself and almost ran to the ladies' room, shoulders shaking with unspent humour all the way there.

He was a man who was obviously used to getting what he wanted and stalked Dianne all night. Every time he managed to get near her, he was all over her like a cheap perfume. Then, he made his biggest mistake and grabbed her bum. Fortunately, I had an unrestricted view of it.

One step too far. Having his silver spoon in his mouth did not entitle him to touch up any girl, never mind mine.

I stormed over, and gave him a Salford handshake. It's similar to a Glasgow Kiss—head smash to the bridge of the nose. There was blood everywhere. Poor Tony was horrified. Somebody called the local constabulary, and I was unceremoniously cuffed and frog marched out straight to Bow Street nick. Wasn't quite the night of comfort and luxury I had hoped for, but it was worth it. Fortunately, Dianne made a complaint to the police about sexual assault by Harrington Potts, and he dropped the case. I was released without charge.

I was lucky it was kept out of the papers, and I came home like the returning hero. Anyone who was in The Parliament Bar that night would know, from now on, not to mess with a Salford lad's girl.

We went back to the hotel to collect our bags—and a few other souvenirs. *Hope you like your birthday present, Mam.*

We laughed and joked all the way back home, and I just knew for once in my life I had made the right choice. I had a funny feeling Dianne's teaching days were over, and I had a new assistant. Hey, who knew, maybe a future wife. Only time would tell, but I was sure we would have a few laughs finding out.

CHAPTER 3   BROWN ENVELOPES

It was coming back up on the train, I realised, the ex-Mayor had got away with it, and I wasn't having it. I realised I would have to get a few friends involved to get the City's money back, that's when I came up with my plan, but I will tell you about that in a bit...

Upon my return, I went back through the books, seeing Salford firms putting tenders in and never winning the work. I had seen one for a firework display in Buile Hill Park, where Pendlebury Pyrotechnics had put a price in for three grand, then I realized a firm in Liverpool had topped their bid at nine grand. Surely this couldn't be right! The more I dug the more I found. Eddie Smythe Joinery had put in a bid for work on a contract in Salford, ten grand below the firm who got the contract. They were from St. Hellens. It just wasn't adding up. I realised we needed that money, and it wasn't going to be sat in Bowarts Bank for long.

I contacted Susan, who I was really beginning to rely on. Without her, I would be lost. My mind was ticking over how I could I get the money back. There was only one way, in my mind. I started to formulate a plan.

I gave Susan a list of numbers I needed to contact, including John "the Mighty" Roberts, his brother, Paul, and my old school mate, Froth. If anyone could get the money back, these boys could. Phone calls were made, and we all arranged to meet in the Station Bar on Church Street in Eccles.

As always, I seemed to buy every round. All I could get off them three were, "We pay your wages so get them in." To be honest, I didn't really mind,

After about eight rounds and me nearly falling under the table drunk, we all came up with the ideal plan.

I told them Ian Bowart and his thirteen little helpers had been cooking the books, and I needed to know the best way to get the money back. Their simple response indicated that I should give them every address, and leave the rest to them.

"Don't worry. My secretary has them all, and you will have them in the morning but let's not use phones. I will have everything dropped off in a letter, and then, when you have them, destroy the evidence." All readily agreed.

The next day, the letter with all the addresses was in the hands of my three trusted new assistants. Within two days, I was greeted at home by my friends, and Ian Bowart.

Ian Bowart said to me it seems I have made a big mistake and here is a cheque for a million and a half pound. I said that is not good it must be a bank transfer, to which he hastily agreed, I wondered what had gone on for him to agree so fast, it was only when the money had been transferred back into the council account that I was to get the full story.
Bowart left my house as fast as he had landed, then the boys went about telling me the story.

It seemed Bowart was sat in on his own when they called around and was swiftly taken away, they told me he had the easy

options or the not so easy option, seems he was determined
to keep his grubby little hand on the money. So John Paul and
Karl decided to tie a rope around his legs and keep lowering him
down over a motorway bridge on the Height. John, decided
it would be a great idea if he kept swinging him and lowering
him with every move, the poor man Bowart, must of been scared
to death, They told me trucks and all sorts were passing and at
one stage he nearly got hit by a ten ton lorry, it was at this stage,
that he decided to scream up to them he would pay every penny
back with interest and make sure his little helpers would do
the same, the bread was coming back home to where it belonged

...

As I was going through the books, I came across a twenty-five million pound outlay for a stadium, which nobody went to and was miles out of the way for everybody. It was then that I decided this burden around the taxpayers' neck must be set free.

I called the chairman of the Salford Reds rugby team, and arranged a meeting. It went something like this, do you want to buy the stadium or our 50% of it for what we paid for it, he said how much, I said give us what it stands us at, and you can have it, he said I will give you 15 million, I said you won't, end of meeting, with this he left.

I had to find another buyer, and that I would. In a meeting with Susan, she came up with the idea of selling it to the class of '92. For all you people who don't know who they are, where have you been, it Giggs the Nevilles Scholes, some great names in Manchester United's history. Well, as I was talking with Susan, she told me Moor Lane was prime building land, and we would get about five million for the plot. I then decided that we would have to build a new ground, and I had the ideal location.

Having watched Salford Reds a few times, I knew there fans were the most loyal in rugby. In my earlier days, I had even travelled abroad watching them.

I had been in Spain, and on the beer for twenty-four hours—you know what it is like when the weather is hot. I knew quite a few of them who were at the game, like Spud Edwards,

Shane "I will tackle anything" Hansen, Wazza Mezza Saundy, Dad, and Liam. Jason Camp, Frankie Birchall, Ray "the Skullcracker" Dixs, and Budgie.

The next day, after the match, and like I said earlier, seemed I had wanted to fight with all the crowd and had a few fights outside a bar. My eye was all split open, but that wasn't the bad thing. I had sharted, if you don't know what that is, it is a cross between a fart and following through. That was the most embarrassing thing in my life, and the coach stunk all the way back to Spain.

The class of '92 had been contacted, and a meeting was arranged. I was to meet my heroes but they weren't getting the ground on the cheap, that was for sure. White elephant or not, we sat down, and a price was agreed; thirty million for our fifty percent, and a promise that they had planning permission for the new hotel and complex that was to be built. I was taking to this job like a duck to water. All I needed now was a new ground, a chairman, and the backing of the fans, which I was confident I would get.

CHAPTER 5   NEW BEGINNINGS

With the ground sold, the Salford Reds chairman, Michael Toukan, *demanded* to see me. I wasn't having that, so, Susan, took the call, and said Toukan wanted to know what I was playing at, selling the ground. I told her to get him in.

The next day, when he arrived at my office, there were no handshakes. I usually asked Susan to brew up; this time I didn't bother. He came bouncing in like a doorman demanding to know why I had sold the ground. I told him I wasn't happy; cuts were being made left, right, and centre, and the vulnerable were suffering. That wasn't happening on my watch. He said he had a good understanding with the last mayor. I explained I could see this, after going through the books, how good an understanding they had. It turned into an argument, with Toukan saying buy me out as chairman, which I did. He told me he had pumped millions into the team. I asked how much. He said five million in two years. I said I will give you one, take it or leave it; he took it.

How the roles were now reversed. It didn't seem that long ago he was trying to have me over. Now, I had the job of finding a board and a new chairperson. I called a press conference. Everyone was there, and I even invited the fans for their views. Within a week of the council now owning the team, I had to set out my plans.

They were for Salford and Swinton to share a ground, and the new ground would be not a stone's throw from the old Willows ground. I had big plans, and they were starting to take shape. I was going to build the new ground in Buile Hill Park, use the old golf course, and only employ Salford labour. Gone were the days when work was going to other contractors from outside the city,

I then went on to speak to the fans and tell them my plans and dreams. The team would now be owned by the fans, the chairman, or woman, would be voted for by the fans. I asked if anyone had any questions.

Leo Murphy was first up, how will this work, I told him the gates would go to the club, we at the council will back you for the first three seasons, to the tune of five million a season, then it is up to you to stand on your own gone will be the days of the blank cheque, it is up to you, the fans and players to make this work, The Manchester Evening News And Salford Reporter seemed excited by my plans. Ian Archer asked how we would decide on the board and the chairman. I said that is up to the public of Salford, who now own the club. I wanted a list of the board members and chairman by Friday, so I could put all the relevant plans in place. The cash was coming back in the City, and everyone seemed happy. It was then that I pulled a master stroke, well, two in one day to be honest.
I sold Moor Lane ground for seven million, two more than what I thought I would get, and the Rugby League decided to move their museum to the one in the park, giving the council an extra half a million pounds a year. It was easy being the mayor, or at least I thought so, until I had to sort out Salford Lad's Club.

CHAPTER 6   HELP FOR THE HOMELESS

Everybody in the music scene knew the cover of the album of The Smiths taken outside the Salford Lad's club. It seemed the building hadn't been used much in recent years, so I went down to Ordsall on a fact finding mission. In reality, my side trip was an excuse to get out of the office while the committee debated on who would be the new Salford Reds' chairperson. I keep going back to the books, but once again I will, I seen that there were supposed to be eight homeless people in Salford, I knew through friends and the previous Government through Austerity it was more like fifty, so the lads club with a bit of cash and hard work would be the idea place to get the homeless of the streets and give them some dignity back.

I contacted Susan to suggest a local charity to help run the place, and straight away she told me about two girls from Salford who went out most nights feeding the homeless. I decided there and then this would be the idea place for them to stay while finding their feet and getting there self-respect back. She told me there name was Coffee 4 Craig, I told her to arrange a meeting, and we would have a chat.

This was arranged, and I found out that Risha had a brother called Craig, who had died on the streets of Cardiff, and there was no help for people who had fell on hard times. Fie told me about Lifeshare, and how each charity helps each other, from St. Paul's on Churchway, with the lovely Mrs. Wyhatt, to the church over the road that puts up thirty people a night.

This, I thought, has got to change, and it would. I then told them about my plans for the Salford Lad's Club, and how once I had the building sorted out they would have to run it, which they agreed. I put them in touch with the building surveyor and made sure they were included in all the aspects of the building work. It would cost alone half a million to make this building right. Lucky I had friends who had squeezed Ian Bowart and his mini little army of merry man to the tune of five million.

Round about this time the loan to the government was paid off in full, transport to the vulnerable had been returned, no more cuts were made, unemployment was falling, mainly due contracts going to Salford workers, and things for the city were really beginning to look up at long last. Then I was to hear tragic news about my friend and the city's MP Tony Flynn.

Dianne woke me up early on Wednesday morning, saying you better come downstairs. At first, I thought with her waking me my luck was going to be in and I was going to get my rent, if you don't know what that means and you ain't from Salford I suggest you ask someone who is...

"What is it?" I asked.

She said, "Get the news on…"

=There, in a house in Worsley, the body of Salford MP Tony Flynn was being carried out. As the news went on, it had seemed he had suffered a massive heart attack, while having sex with two high class hookers, Alex Eve and Lianne Austin, seems he had a thing, and was ready to pay big money for three in the bed sex.

The funny thing is I went to school with the madame, a Kathy Ditchburn. I wonder how she talked her way out of that one. Would have loved to have seen her being interviewed, but, being a Salford girl, she would have given no comment. The news was full of Tony Flynn all day long. I had to even go on television, expressing my deep shock at this tragic event. Les Batty, a good friend of Tony's, was on TV, saying he did great things for this city, and went the way most of us dream to go. It seemed to sum Flynn up as a real Salford lad. Now we needed a new MP, and I still had the problem of who was going to be chairman of the Salford Reds.

The next day, with the papers all full of Tony Flynn, I

decided to get the fans back into the Civic Centre. I knew who had watched the club and who cared about the team, so I made my mind up. Either they told me, or I would tell them. We sat down. There were twenty fans, most of them I knew, and they had voted for me to become mayor. To me, that was just a title. I was on a mission to sort this city out, and that I was going to do. I could have done without Tony Flynn dying, but I was going to do what was best for the city, and the team.

This is how the meeting went: right guys, have you decided, to which they replied no, so I went on to say right who wants to be chairman, with this a Louise Woodward Styles spoke and said I do. "Right," I said any objections, no, right carried you Louise, are the new Chairman. Right Vice Chairman, I nominate Steven Roche any objections, no, Rochie you are now vice chairman. Right I want seven fans on the Board," why seven, they asked, I said "that makes nine and if there is a vote on anything, then it is an odd number." To which they agreed ,the seven were Ray Dix, Lee Murphy, Ken Edwards, Wayne Rimmer, Frank Birchall, Warren Evans and Jason Camp, all sorted in less than an hour.

I, then, told them about how the Council would back them, we will see you right to the tune of five million a season, which will get you the best players for three years only then, you stand on your own, Swinton will receive a million a season so to get them up where they belong and both teams work together in the future, all kids under the age of 16 get in the ground for free,

So, to encourage future fans, I had my vision. The new board shared it. I knew we would get there, and get there we did. The fans of the city bought into the dream, as did the players. Soon, we were becoming the team to beat, even though the new ground was under construction. Everything seemed to be going great, and for the first time since 1969, we were back at Wembley.

CHAPTER 8   GHOST TOWN.

With us being in the first final at Wembley since 1969, the proud Chairperson, Louise Woodward Stlyes, and I led the team out. It seems the whole city was there. The only ones that weren't were the burglars who were having a field day, and the Greater Manchester Police reported a one-hundred percent increase in crime that day.

Well, what can I say about the game? From the first whistle to the last, the Salford team tore into Leeds, playing a mixture of brilliant rugby. The way Rangi Chase passed the ball out was amazing. The forwards took the battle to the Leeds forwards straight from the off, with the captain Harrison Hansen being at the thick off the action. Hock was outstanding, giving his all for the cause, and Adrian Morley had the best game of his career for his own town club. The names on that field would live forever in the memories of all Salford fans. Harrison Hansen, even shared the honour of lifting the Cup with another Salford lad, Adrian Morley. What a great gesture! Harry Livesley, had even travelled over from Australia, said he was visiting his family, but spent two days out of the five over in Wembley. His kids were not happy, but he could not miss the moment, no matter how much the cost was. A real Ordsall lad.

However, like I said earlier, the whole town had turned out and in big numbers. Everywhere was deserted. Even Salford Shopping Centre reported the worst taking ever for a Saturday, but, for the city, it was well worth it. We had won the Cup, and the party was about to start.

Darren Johnson was spotted on TV dancing in the crowd, and it seemed even Swinton fans had come along. Ian Wade and John Kilgraff were there, even though they had their Swinton shirts on under their coats.

With this win, I had to make a hasty phone call to Chapman Holmes Catering. We would celebrate at the Civic Centre, and this time with the money I had made was going toward free beer and food, plus I had a bet on Salford out of the Council Tax Payers Fund at the start of the season at 6 to 1. So I brought the city in another three million, less the cost of the catering for the day, which I knew who be a fair price.

I had to leave Wembley that night to be home for the next day where the team could show the Cup of to the fans. It was a good thing it had already organised, as the team went around the city on an open top bus parade, before getting to the Civic Centre to show the fans the Cup. To say there were thousands there would be an understatement, and I took great privilege in saying, "Here are the 2015 Challenge Cup Winners." There was a massive, ear shattering roar. The players were introduced one by one, and the crowd cheered and cheered some more. All I could say was, I bet there were a few sore heads at work the next morning.

CHAPTER 9   THE NEW MP

With the demise of my old mate, Tony Flynn, we had the lengthy task of finding a new MP. I wanted to find someone who truly cared about the city.

And that was a Yorkshire girl who came here in her teens, and she loved the town from the day she stepped off the bus. She was born in West Yorkshire, a little pit village called Sharlston. She saw so much hardship. Her dad was a miner, like all her uncles, and she loved her family so much, but when she left school, there was no work. Had a couple of jobs, but each time, the businesses had closed down. Along with her friend, she came here to Salford to get work when the pair were sixteen, and never regretted it. One thing about the people of Salford, they made them feel so welcome.

She was now nearly sixty-seven years old, and still carried the same love for Salford that she had when she was younger. To know Salford, you have to live in Salford, and care about the city. And having met all the candidates, there was only going to be one choice for me. Noreen Bailey, a woman with her heart in the right place. I had met all the others, and I knew a good person when I saw one. She stood for all I believed in, and if I could get her to Westminster, I would. I wrote her a cheque out for her Campaign Fund, from the money I had won off the Challenge Cup bet.

I was happy. I had made the right choice, and I knew Noreen Bailey would be a great asset to this city in Westminster, and she would always look after the have nots, rather than they have beens. That was an old Little Hulton saying, when the overspill moved up there in the seventies.

Well, with the campaign funds she had, needless to say, she walked into Westminster, overturning the safe Labour seat. The city was really looking up, and Noreen was to do us proud. The Manchester Evening News described her as a cage fighter in a dress, a real woman of the people. I knew as soon as I saw her, she would do amazing things for the city and always care, like I did. Only, she wasn't as dodgy, and this was about to come and hurt me in a big way.

Three days after the Final, I had been working late in the office, and was going to my car when I was met by Bowart, Toukan, and Pope. Seems I had upset the three of them at some point in my life. Pope was first to speak, he said to me "Payback time", Bowart said "Expect the Unexpected", and Toukan said "Don't be getting no wrong impressions…"

I knew what they meant, and I knew what was coming. What I didn't know was they had been planning this for a long time. Surely my old friend Shazza would have known about this. Who knows, maybe she did, maybe she didn't.

It only felt like about a second as the baseball bat hit me smack in the face, and they proceeded to beat me to a pulp. If it wasn't for Salford City Radio DJ Joe Barnwell, who worked just facing, I would have been dead. He stopped me getting killed by shouting, and then Susan, who could hear the screams, called for an ambulance.

I will never know, to this day, how I lived through the attack.

I had to spend three months in Salford Royal, where I came across my old friend, Nurse Jodie Hookway. After a week of being on a life support machine, and looking like a rotting apple, I could finally open my eyes again. I was greeted by Dianne and Eddie, wanting to know who had done this.

Dianne was more concerned about my health, whereas Eddie and Lee Bamber wanted revenge. As I was lying on the bed, all I could think of was if it wasn't for Susan and Joe Barnwell, I would be dead. The police never got anyone for the attack and seeing as there was CCTV in the Civic Centre, I realised they had help inside as well. I might have cost Toukan and Bowart millions, but I didn't think this was Pope's game. They would pay for this. It would have been easier if they had done the job proper, but they never seemed to do anything right. This would now cost them more than they could possibly imagine.

I had spent that much time in Salford Royal during my life through one thing or another, it was beginning to become like a second home to me. The only thing that changed was the nurses, although Hookway always seemed to be there to give me hassle, instead of comfort. As my time was mostly spent lying down, I was beginning to become friendly with most of the nurses.

Even the staff nurse, Claire, came up to me one day and said, "You know my mam, don't you?"
"Who is that?" I asked.
"Two Builders from Barnsley".
"Oh, yes, I know your mam", I replied.
She said, "You know, she's Dianne Rix".
My mind instantly remembered a bar in Spain.
"You know our kid as well."
"Who is that?"
"Nurse Lauren."
"I bet your mother is so proud of you both." She smiled.

As the weeks were going by, I was becoming friendly, when Dianne wasn't there, with a certain nurse Sarah. It was more to do with her massive chest. The buttons on her uniform always seemed like they were about to pop off. I was just hoping I would be there to see it when it happened, but that was just wishful thinking on my behalf. She would sit and talk, and generally flirt with me, and I would flirt back, only when Dianne wasn't there.

Anyway, as I was getting better and ready to leave, Dianne was sitting at my bedside reading the evening news.

"Oh my god, Si, remember Cuthbert Harrington Potts?" She giggled as I grunted. "I shouldn't laugh; the guy's dead."

I sat up. "How?"

"It says here he was found with his underpants round his ankles and a microwave door embedded in his face…and a can of whipped cream in his left hand. Inside the microwave was what looked like the remains of a watermelon."

"I'd say he got his just desserts."

Dianne laughed. Her whole face lit up when she laughed. Right there and then I thought it would be a good idea if I asked Dianne to marry me. Which she agreed.

I told all the nurses, and they all seemed happy apart from Sarah that is. I told her how I had always liked Dianne, and she seemed to understand, or at least I thought so, then she drew the curtains around the bed, and flashed me the biggest breasts I had ever seen in my life.

"This is what you're missing," she said, and with that, covered them up. "Good luck. I hope you're very happy."

For days, I could not get that image out of my mind.

I broke the news to Susan, who said she would help organise everything with Dianne. Always best to leave women to this sort of stuff, as they like a good wedding. Just foot the bill, I thought. So now I needed a best man, and there was only going to be one: my old mate, Don Bowman. I knew he had moved to sunnier climates, but was sure he would be back as fast as he could. He, like me, enjoyed a good piss up. It wasn't long until he was on the phone to Bob Stephenson and Allan Grundy. As soon as I knew who he had invited, I just knew what a top night we would have. Of that, I had no doubt.

CHAPTER 11   EDDIE'S REVENGE

While I was still in hospital, Eddie had taken it upon himself to get revenge on Pope, Toukan, and Bowart. His mate had been battered to within an inch of his life, and they weren't getting away with that. Eddie soon got his team together, Lee "Mad Dog" Bamber, Scott Dixon, Dave Allen, and even made Phil Howard had come back from Bulgaria on a false passport, so no one knew he was here.

After I told Eddie who had done it, all he would say was leave it with me. I knew he was builder, but I used to smile to myself because all I could think of when he said it was Ted Glen off Bob the Builder. Well it turned out Bowart, Toukan, and Pope were never to be seen again. A week after I left the hospital, Eddie turned up at the Civic Centre, and said, "We're going for a ride."
"Where?"
"Just drive."
I said, "Stop pissing about. Tell me where we are going. This ain't a gangster story."
He replied, "Go to the new development on the old ground." So I drove there.
First thing I said was, "Hasn't this come on?"
With a glint in his eye, he said, "Yes, we've been working hard, sometimes through the night."
"What?"
Flatly, he replied, "You heard, come with me."
So we walked. He then stopped pointed and said, "See

them footings there?" I nodded, "Bowart."

My mouth dropped open. You could have knocked me down with a feather.

I gaped at the spot, with a blank expression on my face. I nearly jumped out of my skin when he said, 'Walk.' We moved along several more steps, and we stopped. He pointed again.

"What?" I asked, almost fearful of the answer.

"Toukan."

I couldn't believe what I was hearing. "Walk". Again, I did as I was told. Again, we stopped; he pointed, and then said the final name, "Pope." I knew what he had done. He said chillingly, "You ever repeat this to anyone, and guess what?"

I honestly believed him. He smiled, and gestured back to the car. When we got back in the car, he conversed as if nothing had happened, and I didn't want to know the story, trust me. All I knew was no matter how much they had done me in, they didn't deserve that.

CHAPTER 12   STAG DOO

Don was in his element organising the stag doo. The night before I had told him about Sarah, so, first thing in the morning he made a bee line to the hospital to invite all the nurses on the ward, especially Sarah. I wasn't sure if I was happy or not, as I felt tight on Dianne, but he said, "It's okay. Last night of freedom, right?"

How true was that statement going to be…

Well, the boys and I headed off for Eccles, always a great drink on Church St, and we seemed to go in every pub there. I was well and truly drunk. I got to the stage where I was singing, "I'm getting married in the morning, ding dong the bells are gunna chime…"

Sarah was a flirt, like me, and I loved it, every second, to be honest. What man wouldn't? A good looking girl carrying on with me, and I was about to be married in a week. As the night wore on, I drank more and more, until I saw an old friend, Billy T.

I can remember this as clear as day. He said, "Hi, Williams. Got you a taxi."

"Nice one, mate." I promptly fell asleep. It was only when I woke up the next morning, in Scotland, I was in a panic. They all thought it would be funny to send me up there. All I had was my phone, and at least I had my clothes on, that was a bonus.

I looked through my phone, and saw I had a friend who lived up there, thankfully! Dianne Wolfenden, Wolfie to her mates, worked on the oil rigs. I just hoped she was on shore. It was six in the morning, and I was freezing my knackers off to be honest. I phoned, and kept it ringing for ages. When she answered, the first words were: "What the fuck do you want at this time?"

I asked her to calm down, and told her the story about how I ended up there. "It's gonna take two hours for me to get to you. Go get yourself in a café, and I'll pay when I get there." She hung up the phone.
"

After walking round Glasgow for an hour I found a café. So I got warm and phoned Billy T., who thought it was funny. Then I rang Don, Bob, and Allan, who was all taking the piss. As I got off the phone, Wolfie came walking in, slapping me across the back of my head for waking her up. She'd just gotten off the rigs after three weeks of nightshift, and didn't go to bed until 3 a.m. After a coffee and a quick catch up, she paid the bill, and I was on my way home at long last, thanks to Wolfie.

It was the week before the wedding, and all I could hear out of Susan and Dianne was, "Oh, that will be lovely." As you can imagine, not a lot of council business got done. They were too busy gossiping, even when Susan put a call through by SHAZZA. She didn't think nothing about it. "Williams, please meet me, I am in turmoil missing my Jonathon. I need to see you please." Stupidly I agreed. I went straight to the car and headed to meet her at the new ground in the park.

Susan and Dianne were too busy talking about weddings to even notice me leave.

When I met her, she looked different, to be honest. She'd lost a lot of weight. I didn't know if she had been on a diet, or if it was worry, but she had definitely lost weight.

"You're looking good," I said.
 "I don't feel it."
"Why?" I asked.
"You know why."
"I don't," I said, stupidly.
She looked me straight in the eye. "You have ruined my life."
"How have I done that?"
"You know how. I was happy in Spain, was getting married to the man of my dreams…"
"Listen," I cut her off. "That bastard tried fitting me up, then my mam. So, yes, in Spain he got what he deserved"
"Yes, I understand that," she said. "But, where is he now? I

am going out of my mind with worry. Please tell me." She started to cry.

I felt sorry for a split second. "You sure you want to know?"

"Yes." Her voice was raspy.

"Get in the car," I told her. We drove to the new development.

She was hysterical, and I sighed. "Please stop it."

She knew. "Where is he?" she asked through the sobs.

I, then, did the stupidest thing of my life. "Here or thereabouts." I started walking the way Eddie took me. I shrugged "Toukan as well, and there is the hat trick, Bowart."

She was balling her eyes out, but she was getting me to admit it, little did I know at the time.

"Yes, I did it. They nearly killed me. Bad mistake. Now they are a part of the new build."

She was clever. "This is all your own work?"

To which I was smirking at her, almost laughing, saying, "Yes, it is all me. Mess with me, and get what is coming to you."

I had turned evil.

"I have seen enough. Take me away."

So I did. We got in the car and drove off. I dropped her at the new ground, even having the cheek to say, "Look after yourself." Little did I know, I would see her again, and very soon, but this time she would be the one laughing.

CHAPTER 14   THE WEDDING

The morning of the wedding, Don, my best man, had woken me up early with Vodka. "You need a drink."

Susan had spent the night at ours, getting everything ready for the following day. I had my best suit on, and if I say so myself, I didn't look too bad.

I was getting married at the Civic Centre. Don and I got there early, and the guests were already arriving.

I spoke with the vicar, Neil Edward. He seemed a good man, and I knew he would not let us down. Dianne arrived, and she was the vision of beauty, amazing. I looked at her, and I knew I had made the right choice.

As Don passed me the ring, the doors suddenly burst open. There stood the Greater Manchester Police. I never did get the chance to marry Dianne. One walked up to me.
"Williams, I am arresting you for the murders of Toukan, Bowart, and Pope."
"What?"
"You heard!"
"I heard what you said." Just then I saw Shazza, who said, "Remember first time I came to yours, and you checked me for wires?"
I thought there and then on the spot, *Oh fuck. They have me bang to rights.* So they did.

As they lead me away, I was in a state of shock, my nearly new wife, Dianne was in floods of tears. All my friends at the wedding were staring. The police lead me to a waiting car and drove me to the Crescent Police Station, where my solicitor was waiting. If anyone could help, it would be good old Rainford, but even this might be a little too much for him. Three missing people, presumed murdered, in the footings of the old Willow's Ground. They were going to have some digging to do, and they weren't going to get any help from me.

After spending four hours in the interview room and hearing them playing the tape over and over again, they finally got fed up with me saying, 'no comment.' There were the usual questions, and the odd sarcastic comment going both ways. I always try to give as good as I got when dealing with GMP's finest. They asked about their old mates, Pope, Toukan, and Bowart. The answer was mainly, 'no comment,' as I only knew what Eddie had told me. It was important to have a word with him, but, as usual, they weren't letting me have any visits. I saw the Daily Mirror, and I was all over the front page, sure I pushed their sales up that week tenfold.

After keeping me in the station for seventy-two hours, they finally transferred me back to Gameways, where I was met by an old cockney screw, Paul Wilson.

"Would you Adam and Eve it, Williams the Mayor. Oh, three murders. Not looking good this time, is it?" he said, and started laughing.

So we went through the same old routine as usual, chest size large, waist 32, long legs on the pants, and then the old classic, underpants triple XL, just to see his face. I didn't know why I said it. Maybe because he was taking the piss.

"You're never triple XL."

"Ask the wife, and how is she?"

To say he wasn't impressed would be an understatement, but such is life. I had been through this routine a few times, and they knew it. They weren't getting one over on me, and every little battle won is a result, but at least while on remand, I would be on visits, and I could find out what was happening.

First to see me was Dianne. She had never been in a place like this before, and it was a big culture shock to her to be honest. She was sat at the table, crying, as I walked over, with my jeans, sweatshirt, and bib on. We spoke, and she asked me if I did it. I told her, "No, I didn't."

"They have you on tape admitting it all. It has been leaked to the papers."

"Oh really," I said, knowing they had a conversation between me and Shazza that didn't prove anything, and would never stand up in court.

After an hour, which seemed like five minutes, it was time for Diannc to leave. I her to make sure she get in touch with Eddie, and got him to come and see me as soon as he could. Dianne told me he had been acting all strange, and kept asking to see me. I said to tell him to call on his own, and make sure it was the next visit. We kissed, and she said she would.

Two days passedm and after seeing old Rainford and going through my optionsm it wasn't looking very good, to be honest. I really did need to see Eddie.

At long last, I saw Eddie. I had so many questions I had been banged up for a week. So as soon as we sat down, I started to fire them off. It went something like this. "Fucking hell, mate, I am looking at three life sentences here. What the fuck have you done to me? Dianne is a mess and what about the kids? And where do I go from here, mate?"

All Eddie was doing was smirking and saying, "Don't worry. You will be out soon, with a load of compo, but just wait till they dig the new footings up."

"Wait," I said "What the fuck you on about?"

He grinned. "It is all under control, just leave it with me."

"These bastards have got me bang to rights, and all you can say is leave it with you?"

"Look," he kept saying. "You will be out soon, trust me."

I snapped, "I better fucking be. I am getting far too old for this entire jail lark, mate. The screws keep taking the piss, saying, 'Not the chains your used to, eh, Williams?' thinking there being witty. Dianne, crying all most constantly, and I ain't seen the kids either. Just tell me what is going on."

"No," Eddie replied firmly. "All I will say is you will be out soon, trust me."

I had no choice; I had to trust him. He then went on to ask what the plod was saying, to which I replied, "Oh, the usual. I said old faith, no comment, for seventy-two fucking hours, no thanks to you. Whatever did you take me to the new ground for and tell me what you had done." He smirked yet again. "What have you done about that bitch Shazza setting me up?"

"She is walking around giving it the big 'un."

"Oh and your letting all this happen?" I replied angrily.

All he kept saying was, 'don't worry, you will be out soon,' and for once I had to believe him. I needed a bit of hope. I was looking at the rest of my life in the big house, and I didn't really fancy that. To say I was getting stressed would be a bit of an understatement. All Eddie kept saying was, 'you will be ok.' Finally, I snapped and said, "For fuck sake, tell me what is going on."

He calmly smiled and said, "Right, okay, mad arse."
"Mad arse, you fucking tell me, will you?"
"Right, okay, I will," he said "Right, the plod are digging the new footing up again. Going to cost a fucking fortune. They have got about three plots to go, and should be finished by Friday. Then, I will let Toukan go. He has whinged the most, so he can go first."
My eyes went wide, as my jaw dropped open. "What?"
"I never buried them alive. I took them to the docks and locked them up in a container, like sardines in a can."
"How long have they been there?"
"Seven weeks," Eddie replied.
"Fuckin' hell, Eddie, are you losing it?"
"No I just wanted the bastards to suffer, and big time, so like I said, just chill out for a few more days and Toukan will be released."
I was in total shock, but buzzing as well. They weren't going to bang me up for the rest of my life. It would only be days before I would be out. I went back to my cell with a massive smirk on my face on my face. Not only had they dug my mam's garden up in the past, that was nothing to what this was going to cost them.

CHAPTER 17   LAZURUS TIMES THREE

A couple of days after my visit with Eddie, the police called to ask me some questions. They wanted to know where the bodies were, as if I was going to say. I just sat there smirking, knowing sooner or later they would have to let me out.

It was during this interview, the police told my solicitor, "We need to have a word outside."

Rainford went outside and came back, smiling, "It seems Toukan has been found walking in a daze around Weaste."

"Oh really," I said. "So three now becomes two?" I looked at the police. "So I suppose that's a charge dropped then, eh?"

They looked angry, and even told me to, "atop taking the piss."

"You're the ones taking the piss. An innocent man banged up, all because of a stupid conversation with a girl who robbed me for thirty grand, spending my money with your mate, Pope, buying a bar in Spain. I haven't a clue where they are, and how's the digging going?" With this, they left, and then Rainford and I had a few words.

"Off the record, where are the others?"

I trusted him, and told him, "They are still alive, and will be out walking the streets soon enough."

"Right, I will have these for wrongful arrest, and as soon as they are...found, you will be out."

Four hours later, Bowart was spotted in Eccles again, walking in a daze, and lastly, Pope was dropped off in Kersal, also in a daze. They hadn't seen any light for nearly eight weeks, so you can imagine how they must have been squinting. Within hours of this, it seemed Rainford had been to the High Courts, and I was released, three counts of murder dropped, and when the gates of the prison opened, it seemed every newspaper in the world was there.

My eyes felt like how theirs must of felt, with the amount of cameras going off. It was then I did my speech. "I fully understand the work of GMP, and I realise their enquires must continue in the tragic kidnapping of these three gentlemen, but this was a clear case of me being fitted up, and my solicitor will be seeking compensation for this miscarriage of justice, not to mention ruining my wedding day. Hopefully, this matter will be sorted soon". I was hastily put into a car, and driven home to my fresh sheets and a very happy Dianne. It was going to be a night to remember, in more ways than one.

We had only been apart for a week, but it felt like months. I couldn't believe we made it home without crashing the car. Dianne kept brushing my leg when she changed gear. It felt like electricity shooting through every nerve ending in my body. Dianne looked across and smiled at my ever tightening trousers.

"Bloody hell, Williams. You have missed me." She laughed. "I better get you home before you have someone's eye out with that."

My inner god was cartwheeling, back-flipping and getting hornier by the second.

As we turned into the drive, I saw two journalists and Mrs. Foster from a few doors down loitering near my front door.

"Bollocks." There was one thing and one thing only on my mind, and it wasn't a quick chat with the press or nosey neighbours.

"You can't get out of the car like that," said Dianne. "Can you imagine your mother seeing a picture of her son with a stiffy on the front page of *The Advertiser*? She would be mortified!"

"Don't be daft. She's seen it all before."

"Not as solid as that I hope, Simon! Just cover it up, or think of something else to distract you. Think of football."

I sat back, letting my inner god put on his United kit and walk out of the tunnel into the theatre of dreams. The noise from the crowd was deafening.

"Are you thinking about, Giggs? 'Cos it's getting bigger."

Dianne laughed.

"Bollocks. I should have thought about Rooney. Look, it's not going to work. I'll just cover it up." I looked round to see if there was anything on the back seat. Empty apart from my mam's wedding hat. "That'll do nicely."

We got out of the car and headed up the path, my mam's wedding hat saving my embarrassment.

"Simon! Anything you want to say to our readers about the events leading up to your stint at Her Majesty's?"

"No comment, fellas. Look, it's been a long week, and I just want to sit down on my own couch and have a brew. There will be a press release tomorrow." The two hacks decided to take a few snaps anyway. I wasn't happy about having a picture of me carrying a bright yellow feathered hat. No self-respecting Salford lad would be seen dead carrying that, but it was better than my manhood standing to attention for all the world to see. I almost got away with it.

"Awww, Simon, love. Lovely to see you back home. Have they let you off then? Come 'ere, Willibobs, give us a welcome home cuddle."

In the blink of an eye, Mrs. Foster had thrown her arms around me and gripped me in a head lock that Hulk Hogan would have been proud of. For one unfortunate split second, I forgot the hat and responded with a warm embrace. "Thanks, Mrs F. It's good to be home." I pulled away from her and turned to go into the house. There were howls of laughter as I did. The camera taking rapid fire shots. Even Dianne had tears streaming down her face. "What? What are you laughing at?" The words had barely left my mouth when I looked down and realised the hat was still there, hanging on to my knob like it was a clothes peg!

As I ran into the house, I heard Mrs. Foster shout. "Blimey, lad, you are excited about being home…"

No sooner had I walked through the doors then Dianne put her arms around me, kissing me like she had never done before. Slowly my hands were all over her, kissing her in the places I knew turned her on. I was nibbling at her ear, and I knew that did it for her. My lips touched hers, and she was breathing heavily. I was sucking her lip, and she soon released my pants. They fell to the floor.

Her skirt was hastily unzipped. We were naked, kissing, and we didn't even wait to get upstairs. I had over a week of pent up frustration, and it was going to be released. I had the feeling she was the same. Her hands slowly felt the whole of my naked body. She reached the spot where she knew I was in heaven, and took the lot into her wide mouth. With each suck and lick, she moved onto my face, and the act was repeated on her. This went on several hours. Before long, I could see the light of the morning shining through the windows.

The next day, I stayed off work to avoid the press, but I couldn't have done much anyway. I had no energy. Dianne had drained me, and that was probably the best night of my life, like my lotto ticket had come in. That wasn't only thing to come, trust me on that one…

The End, or is it…

Printed in Great Britain
by Amazon

53036268R00110